CW00481422

THE DECISIONS WE MAKE

Young Adult, M/M Gay Romance

RJ SCOTT

Love Lane Books

The Decisions We Make

All Rights Reserved

Always for my family.

THE
DECISIONS
WE
MAKE

RJ SCOTT

Love Lane Books

Chapter One

Then

"Do you think he loves *Star Wars* or crappy Transformers like Mark?" Sue Walker looked down at her middle child and smiled at his question. His bright blue eyes shone with excitement, and he hopped from foot to foot. Jamie never actually sat still for anything longer than ten minutes in any one go. Not even when he played video games; he was constantly on the move in his seat.

Jamie was the most laid-back of her children. Nothing ever appeared to faze him. He was comfortable in his own skin—athletic, above average bright, and just a very happy open child. Sue had wanted more children after Megan, he youngest, but an emergency operation after her daughter was born meant no more children for her. That didn't mean her heart had stopped wanting more though, and when Megan turned two, Jamie nine, and Mark thirteen, that was when she'd spoken to Don about fostering. He agreed immediately. They were financially secure, and Sue wasn't alone in wanting a large family.

She and Don, her husband of twenty years, had sat all three kids down and explained they wanted to put themselves forward as a foster family. There was no sense in agreeing to care for a new child if her own family was hesitant. Sue was honest with them all, and one by one, her family told her it was a wonderful idea. She couldn't have been prouder of a single one of them. Mark, her eldest, who asked if they could get a girl with boobs. Her middle boy, Jamie, who needed reassurance he wouldn't have to share his room. Lastly, her youngest, Megan, who was just worried it would be yet another boy. All three were excited in different ways to add to their family.

So today, it was happening. Their first foster placement would be here soon, and his name was Daniel Keyes. The authorities had explained he was quiet, shy, and a gifted kid, one who needed love and attention to make him blossom as a child. Sue had patience and love to spare. She was determined Daniel would be safe here.

"He's only four months younger than you, so I'm sure he will love *Star Wars*." Wasn't that what most nine-year-olds liked at the moment? It was certainly what Jamie adored.

Jamie took the news in stride, and she loved him for it. Feeling secure was never an issue for Jamie Alexander Walker.

"An' he's not staying forever?"

"No. Fostering means he will stay just as long as he needs to until a new family is found for him."

"And I really don't have to share my room?"

"No. Dad is setting up a bed in the spare room."

The wide grin that Jamie gave her was confirmation enough he was happy about that situation. She only hoped her other two were as easy to win over. Daniel, the boy they were going to be given, was an orphan. He'd lost his father to cancer and his mother to apparent suicide. He was going to be a more than a little lost and lonely nine-year-old, and it would be Jamie's good nature that took the brunt of any emotional problems Daniel might have. Being the same age meant the same class at school and similar interests.

"So the only thing he'll use is the den?" Jamie looked up at her. The den was Jamie's domain, where Vader battled with Luke and Han flew to the rescue. Sue nodded and then dropped to her knees in front of Jamie. The den had been taken over by the arrival yesterday of a piano.

"Daniel plays the piano, and apparently, he is very good at it. It will be great for him to have something he can have here that is his." She subsided into thought at the worry of just how damaged Daniel might be by everything he had seen in his short life.

"I'm really excited about him coming. Please don't be sad," Jamie offered gently. Sue realized her son had picked up on her sudden quiet mood, and she hugged him tight. He might be a bundle of excitable drama, but under it all, he really was the most sensitive of her kids.

"I'm fine, sweetie. Are you going to meet him at the door with me?"

"How long is it gonna be?"

"Ten minute's time."

"'Kay, Mom. I'm going to check his room and make sure it has some more good stuff in it."

Mark was away at football practice, and Megan was at a party for a friend. It was just her and Don and Jamie. Jamie was back at her side, peering out through the frosted glass of the front door. He couldn't keep still and was again hopping from foot to foot with excitement.

"Calm down, sweetie; Daniel is kind of shy," she warned him.

"Okay, Mom, I'll try." If Jamie had any faults, it was that he had an overabundance of confidence, enthusiasm, and general all round hyperactivity. They weren't a family that could be labeled as quiet by any stretch of the imagination. They were a boisterous crowd, but social services said that would be good for Daniel, and when Sue was handed Daniel's file, her heart just melted.

The car pulled up, and a short boy, dark hair flopping over his eyes, a bag clutched in long fingers, stepped out of the vehicle and stood uncertainly, looking up at his new house. He spotted Sue, and a small smile crossed his face, then he turned, exchanging words with his companion, before nodding and holding onto her hand. He lowered his head as he neared the door, not lifting it even as Sue welcomed his placement officer and him in. He just scuffed his feet on the doormat.

"Hello, Daniel," Sue said brightly. She noticed her son had stopped hopping from foot to foot and instead was staring at the new boy. She could feel him visibly bristling with excitement but trying to keep it inside.

"'Lo," came the soft reply, still no eye contact.

"Why don't you let Jamie show you your room, Daniel?" his mom said.

Daniel lifted his gaze, his gray eyes filled with an expression of fear. Sue wanted to say something clever to dispel the young boy's fears, but Jamie interrupted in his usual take-no-prisoners fashion.

"Yeah, Daniel, come with me and see. We got like painted bits, and posters, and I didn't know what you was bringin', but I put like loadsa books in your room and some *Star Wars* stuff and some trading cards. I mean they're the ones I have two of, but you know you can always swap 'em if you already have 'em, and I've also got like this second controller for you to play with me. Come on. Quick."

Jamie grabbed at Daniel's arm, just reaching farther as Daniel backed away a bit startled at the touch, and giving him no chance to argue, Jamie dragged him up the stairs.

Chapter Two

D ANIEL LET HIMSELF BE DRAGGED ALONG BY THIS BOY CALLED
Jamie, who pulled him into a room at the end of the corridor at
the corner of the house, overlooking the yard and with views of
California hills. It was far from a large room, but it held a bed
that looked soft and welcoming, and just like he'd said, Jamie
had put posters of people up on Daniel's wall. Not sheet music,
not a pinboard of timetables and practices, but some guys in
uniform with a ball. Basketball, Daniel thought. What team he
wasn't sure. He didn't actually know a whole lot about sports,
and the idea of a contact sport where he might hurt his hands had
always scared him. Well, scared his mom anyway. Athletics,
group games, had inevitably clashed with extra practice for this
recital or that exam. The boy—Jamie—dropped to the bed,
waving a hand and enthusiastically indicating the whole room.

"Whaddya think?" he said.

Daniel thought he detected excitement, and swallowing,
he pasted a smile on his face and hoped he looked
enthusiastic enough for what he had been given.

"It's fine," he said gently.

Don't cause trouble. It's only for a few months. You can do this, you can talk to people, you can form words and look happy, you know you can because you have been practicing in front of a mirror.

"Cool, wanna play Madden?" the boy asked, crossing to the room opposite his and coming back with a gray box trailing wires, tripping into the room with a broad grin.

"I'm a bit tired," Daniel said softly. That answer always worked now. Those few words were guaranteed to get sympathy and were a surefire way to get people to leave him alone.

"Okay." If the boy was upset he didn't show it. He just dumped the confusion of wires on Daniel's bed and flopped down after it, sprawling completely over the quilt.

Daniel coughed and looked at the boy, at his height, his long, lanky arms and legs, with his short, spiky blond hair and his smile. What was his name again? Jamie. It didn't go down well to not remember names. But with a head full of music, things like names weren't a priority. Okay. He could do this.

"Where's my piano?" Daniel asked softly, his voice a little husky from lack of use.

"Oh yeah, it was delivered on this huge ass truck, and they were swearing and everything when they put it in my den. Well, like, it's not my den now. It's your den. Whatever, come on then." Jamie started to leave the room, looking back expectantly. Daniel blinked then followed, down the stairs, past the kitchen where Sue and the social worker sat drinking coffee, and through a door at the back, leading out to flooding sunshine and warmth.

And there she was, standing in the corner, his only real link to his parents.

He crossed to her and sat on the seat, running fingers over highly polished wood.

He was aware of Jamie watching him curiously.

This is wrong.

He and the piano both belonged in shadows and musty rooms, rooms that his music stayed in, rooms where he felt safe. Sitting in sunlight, breathing in California air, was all wrong.

He wouldn't be able to play here. That much was certain.

If he couldn't play, he wouldn't be happy.

It's only for a few months.

He just wouldn't play.

It will kill me, but it won't be for long.

Jamie looked at Daniel, his head to one side. "You going to play?" he said curiously.

Daniel didn't look up even as Jamie launched into more words.

"'Cause Ellie can play like this Chinese thing, and she got up and did it in 'sembly, and it was rubbish. 'Cause like, Ellie, she has this piano at home, and she has this man come over and show her how to play, and she has had lessons for three years, and if that Chinese thing is all she can play, then that is just rubbish."

Daniel looked up at the boy who couldn't seem to stop talking, blinking at him from under his long fringe. "I'm not going to play," he said softly.

"Oh." Jamie looked flummoxed and then frowned. "Why?"

"I can't—"

"My mom said you might not play 'cause your mom died. Is that why? Megan likes nursery rhymes so can you play them? Josh likes rock. It's really noisy, and I kind of hate it, but I guess if you can only do that Chopsticky Chinese thing, then other stuff would be way too hard. Can you do nursery rhymes... hmmm?"

"It's too sunny in here," Daniel blurted out. The talking that Jamie was throwing at him had started to sound too confusing—just a jumble of noise. Nobody talked to him like that; they talked quietly and firmly and didn't make him want to talk back at all. No one mentioned his mom being dead. Or his dad.

"Huh?" Jamie looked confused, looking out of the window. "We can play *Star Wars* in here, and yeah, sometimes it gets hot with the sun, but not all the time. Maybe you can go under the piano and just play the pedally things at the bottom? It would be cool under there."

"I ... I can't... can't play, the sun... it's not right."

"Okay. So under would be a good idea? I think that's a good idea. I get ideas all the time. Well, mostly good. 'Cepting the time I broke my ankle jumping off the garage roof. Hang on, I got an really cool one."

Daniel didn't move one inch. He was absolutely frozen to the spot with confusion. Jamie left the sunroom and then bounded back in to a startled Daniel.

He busied himself, placing the items he had collected on the floor under the piano, and then popping back up, a huge grin split his face.

"Get under here, Daniel; it's dark under here." He looked at Daniel expectantly.

"I can't," Daniel said, feeling his chest tighten with anxiety. He was wearing his best pants. His mom wouldn't have liked it if he got dirty when wearing his best pants let alone the cream shirt with the clip tie. Then his new mom, the pretend one, she would be cross, and then everything would be ruined.

"Come on, s'fun. I have Oreos," Jamie wheedled and shook the bag of cookies in encouragement.

"My clothes," Daniel said helplessly.

"What?" Jamie asked with a frown.

"They'll get dirty."

"S'ok," Jamie started, and then cupping his hands round his mouth, he yelled so loud Daniel was sure that people outside heard it. "Mom, can Daniel play in the den with me in his best stuff?"

There was a pause; Daniel didn't know what he wanted Mrs. Walker to say. If she said yes, then this meant Daniel had no excuses not to get on the floor; something he had not really done before.

"Of course he can," came the reply from the kitchen.

Oh no.

"See, Danny, can I call you Danny? 'Cause you can call me Jamie. Come under with me, and then, d'ya want a cookie?"

Daniel swore the other boy's words were running into one another. Still he gathered all his reserves of bravery and slid off the piano chair and under the piano. It was kind of dark, and Daniel had never seen the underneath of any of his pianos before so it was a bit intriguing.

"Cookie?" Jamie crossed his legs, leaning back against one of the piano legs and holding out squashed cookies.

"Okay," Daniel said softly. Cookies were not often on his menu, and the last time he had had one, it had been at his mom's funeral because no one told him he couldn't have one. He bit into the dark chocolate biscuit, his tongue poking out to gather stray crumbs as they collected at the corner of his mouth, brushing others from his pants.

"Wanna see what I can do?" Jamie asked conspiratorially,

darting a quick glance out from under the piano. "It's a secret though."

"Okay."

"Promise you won't say?"

"I won't say." Unless he really needed to.

"Solo-swear?"

"What?"

"Solo-swear. Means like you have to be Han Solo and you can't tell no one what you see."

"Okay I… er… Solo-swear… I won't say a word." Daniel wondered if this is what all families in the real world were like, with stupid promises and sitting on dusty floors in best clothes.

Jamie grinned, that goofy, sparkling-eyed, happy-with-the-world grin and proceeded to push a whole cookie in his mouth in one go, looking kind of like the hamster Daniel's English class had babysat for a whole term. Crumbs flew everywhere as the poor cookie met its demise in the cavern that was Jamie's mouth, and Daniel just watched, totally fascinated.

Finished, Jamie leant forward, his eyes intense. "Betcha can't do that," he said, throwing the challenge into the den.

Daniel swallowed. This was a new feeling inside him, a small nagging push to prove Jamie wrong, but it was quickly squashed by the overwhelming need to not do anything stupid.

"I can't," Daniel said finally.

Jamie just dropped back, his face a picture of win, and he began munching on his next cookie. Clearly realizing Daniel was still nibbling on his first, he emptied half of what was left in the packet into Daniel's lap.

This Jamie? He seemed really cool. A bit odd but cool.

Daniel looked from Jamie to the crumbly sticky cookies

in his lap, hoping he could keep his pants clean and cataloguing Jamie in his mind as being ever so slightly scary and ever so slightly odd.

When they were finally made to come out from under the piano, they were both covered in dust bunnies and chocolate, and they had learned a lot about each other.

Daniel had learned that Jamie loved drama, art and playing basketball. Daniel also found out that Jamie had a girlfriend, Tina, she was only eight, but she had a mom who, on a daily basis, sent her to school with a decent supply of candy, hence Jamie's attraction.

Jamie learned that yes, Daniel could play chopsticks and some other stuff with really long sounding names, no, he didn't have a girlfriend, no, he couldn't swim, and horror of horrors, he had never even watched basketball, let alone played it.

What really marked the difference in them as children was *Star Wars*.

Jamie had everything; the quilt cover, *Star Wars* curtains, action figures (including the Boba Fett with removable head; Daniel didn't like to point out that to him it just looked broken), DVDs, books, sticker albums… the list was endless. He could quote parts of the movies verbatim, and in fact did so on a regular basis, much to Daniel's confusion. He even tried to encourage Daniel to play *Star Wars* under the piano, but it was at this point Daniel had to admit the terrible truth.

He had never seen *Star Wars*, none of them, ever, not once, not in the entire nine years he had been alive.

Jamie looked alternately horrified and gleeful. Horrified that Daniel had somehow missed this vital part of his education, gleeful that he could start from the beginning and educate Daniel himself.

Under the piano, Jamie began to plot with Daniel, or

rather plot while Daniel listened, the plans for the great stealing of Mark's prize Optimus Prime, the first Jamie-Daniel prank on the older brother that Daniel hadn't even met yet.

It was planned with so much excitement that Daniel was caught up in it, forgetting he was in a foster home with no parents and with no real long-term plans in place for him. He became embroiled in Jamie's world, and with no holding back, Jamie started to build a new family around him, a family with a mom, a dad, a sister and two brothers.

Scary.

Chapter Three

Now

SIX FEET OF SWEATING, LAUGHING JAMIE DOVE INTO Daniel's room, shutting the door behind him and flicking the lock. An irate Mark pounded up the stairs and banged on Daniel's door seconds behind him.

"Jamie, get your ass out here now so I can kill you."

His eyes full of laughter, Jamie snorted, flopping down on Daniel's bed. "I made it in here, dude; you can't touch me." It was an unwritten rule between brothers that, in the years he had been with them, Daniel's room was "home". There was muttering outside the door, veiled threats and then more banging before Mark stomped down the stairs.

"Hey, Dan." Jamie finally acknowledged him.

Glowering, Daniel sat at his desk, which was littered with books. He fixed his gaze firmly on his foster brother and the sweat rubbing off of him and onto Daniel's clean quilt.

"Get your skinny ass off my bed."

"Two hours practice and a run home; I am fucked, can't move."

"You might as well go now and get the beating over and done with 'cause he's going to get you when you leave, you idiot."

"Nah, I've got you to back me up."

"Uh huh, calculus and geography. Some of us need to work to get to college."

"I work."

"On your jump."

"I have a good average."

"Without trying. Imagine what would happen if you actually tried."

"I try." Jamie looked a bit hurt. School was an easy journey for him and Daniel both, but Jamie chose to let it ride, sailing close to the wind sometimes but always scraping through. Daniel, on the other hand, worked hard and had an impressive average, one guaranteed to get him into a good school.

"You're an idiot, Walker."

"Says the guy studying on a summer day when the hoops are calling."

"And exactly what did you do to Mark now to make him wanna kill ya?"

"Changed the ringtone on his cell to the Muppets."

"Uh huh."

"And then phoned him in the middle of a lecture."

"Jeez, Jamie, not the English lecture with that girl?"

"Yeah."

"You are a complete ass."

"Yeah, but can you imagine Mark I'm-so-popular Walker and his unrequited love in the same room as a Muppets ring tone?" Jamie snorted, and Daniel couldn't help but laugh. Yeah, that would have been kind of funny. "Anyway, like I said, you got my back, and he's scared of you."

"Dude, he's like half a foot taller than me and built."

"Nah, it's the woobly eyes and lips of doom and misery that get him."

"The what?"

"The woobly eyes and lips of doom."

"You so just made that up."

"Yeah, but it kind of fits. One look at your woobly gray eyes and Mark is scared."

"You are kind of an idiot, Jamie."

"It has been said, it has been said." Jamie smirked "Little bit of one-on-one?"

"Like being beaten thirty to two is something I enjoy."

"Hey, you got two. Trust me, Shorty; that is good."

"We can't all be long-armed Gigantors."

"So?" Jamie sounded hopeful.

"Calculus, dude." Daniel sighed. He hated calculus, couldn't see the point of it, and didn't have Jamie's instinctive enjoyment of numbers.

Jamie huffed and leaned over his shoulder. "5%, 3.14, xy, there, done."

"Thanks, but I need the proofs that go with it."

"I'll do it with ya later." Jamie's voice changed to a whine. "C'mon, dude, let's go and work off all the crap we eat."

"The crap *you* eat."

"Whatever… c'mon."

Somehow Daniel got talked into it, got pulled and pushed and finally stood facing a loose-limbed confident Jamie. He bounced the ball, visualizing shooting the hoop… one, feign to the left, two, actually go right, snaking past Jamie's defenses, three aim and shoot, score a net, taking the score to a glorious fourteen-one. Problem was he missed and Jamie grabbed the ball getting the shot and whooping with glee.

Daniel sprawled on his back huffing and sweating and grimacing, even getting to one point was so not working.

Jamie sprawled next to him, grinning. "Fifteen to zero, a new Walker record."

Daniel couldn't even string two words together for a comeback, let alone anything remotely witty.

"Jamie, you little freak!"

Shit, Mark.

Jamie jumped to his feet, laughing as Mark launched himself round the corner and the two fell into an impromptu wrestling match on the grass. Mark definitely had the upper hand, finally pinning his giggling brother by his arms to the ground.

"Uncle, uncle." Jamie couldn't breathe for the laughing.

"Say you're sorry," Mark pushed, a serious expression on his face.

Daniel wished Jamie would stop with the laughing. He was sure it wasn't going down too well with his brother.

"I'm sorry, I'm sorry," Jamie finally croaked out.

Mark rolled off him, lying sprawled next to him, a superior smirk on his face. "Turns out, little brother, Sarah loves the Muppets."

And then the two just lay back, looking up at blue sky, laughing like loons.

Neither noticed when Daniel left.

Chapter Four

Dinner was the normal loud affair, Mark still griping at Jamie, Jamie teasing Megan, and then Jamie and Mark both doing the big brother thing when Megan revealed she liked a boy in her class. To be fair, Daniel also felt a protective rush when he heard the news, and if anything needed to be done to protect her, then Daniel would be there with her brothers. Megan had a very special place in his heart; she was his little sister and had been from the first day she handed him a half-eaten yoghurt, informing him he could have it if it made him stop crying.

"I'm nine now, you know. I am allowed a boyfriend," she protested, looking to Daniel for support. Daniel shrugged, looking to Jamie, and then back to Megan.

"How old is he?" he asked curiously

"He's ten," she said proudly, "and he wants to hold my hand on the playground and everything, and it's great," she finished with a flourish and a what-you-going to-do-about-it attitude

"What's his name?" Jamie wanted to know

"I'm not telling you his name," she replied loftily.

"Ten-year-old boys are only after one thing," Mark started to point out, but stopped at his dad's warning cough.

"Yeah," Jamie continued in his place, "your candy, Megs. He'll want all your candy."

"Ha ha," she snorted, but actually did look a little bit worried. She rivaled Jamie in the whole stuffing-your-face-with-food-until-you're-sick contest. Candy was important to her.

"Jamie, did you choose your team yet?" Sue asked, changing the subject. She always rode to the rescue when Megan was the focus of her three brothers, and basketball was always a good subject. Both Mark and Jamie were players, Mark in college; Jamie in high school. In fact, Jamie was captain of the school team and also heading for a college scholarship based on his skills.

"Yeah, mostly, I mean Grangeville has a strong team, so we have to be careful. Their defense is made up of the guys that…"

Daniel zoned out, as he often did when talk turned to basketball, even though he loved the game. Who couldn't love it when you lived with the Walkers? He supported the school's team, Jamie's team, but really, at the moment, he had more important things on his mind.

He was miserable and had a whole montage of confusion and worry with so many new thoughts swirling around in his brain it made thinking about anything else almost impossible.

Not really listening to what they were saying gave him time to scan the faces around the table.

Mom and Dad, as he now called them after years of religiously using Sue and Don… Well, they would take his news okay. They weren't actually his parents and, in fact, really had nothing they could say. It wasn't as if they were going to throw him on the street, and if they did, he had money—a nest egg of life insurance from his parents. Megan wouldn't even understand what he was going to say, so she was okay. Mark was an unknown quantity, but Daniel decided he'd cross that bridge when he came to it.

It was Jamie he worried about. Jamie who hugged him and tussled with him and slept on his floor and was constantly showing brotherly affection in public. Shit.

A small silence fell between subjects, and Daniel thought it was better to get it out in the open, so he could deal with the fallout now.

"Can I say something?" Five pairs of eyes turned to him. It wasn't often Daniel spoke at the table, preferring to fulfill the role of listener, but at least when he did say something, his family tended to listen. He swallowed, sure he was going bright red. "I'm erm… not sure how to say this to all of you."

"Go on, sweetheart," Sue said gently.

Misery churned in his stomach. Every single thought he had about what and who he was sat heavy on him. He knew who he was—he just didn't expect others to understand.

"First off, I want you to know, if you want me to go after I tell you this, I can. I don't expect you to have to deal with it or accept it or…" He dropped his eyes, fear curling in his stomach.

"What?" Sue finally prompted after a long pause. "What's wrong? What is it, Daniel?"

Daniel lifted his gaze. Tears pricked his eyes, and he was feeling really stupid and tongue-tied at not being able to say what he wanted.

"I think I'm…" *Spit it out.*

"You think what, darling?" Sue said again, so understanding, so strong.

"I think I'm, no… not think… I *know* I'm gay."

Silence.

Broken only by Mark snorting Diet Coke over his dinner.

Daniel looked quickly around at his family, his stomach knotting because no one was saying anything.

Not one person said anything for at least ten seconds. It seemed like hours.

"Thank you for telling us, Daniel," his not-real-mom said softly, reaching over to grasp his sweaty hand in hers, squeezing it softly. She was more of a mom to him in that one simple sentence and that one simple touch than his own mom had ever been.

"Are you sure you are, Daniel?" Don, forever with the practicalities.

"I'm sure; I've been sure for a very long time," Daniel said quietly.

"Then I'm glad you told us," he replied. "You realize this won't be an easy path through life, Daniel."

"I know." God, he knew well what barriers and hate he would have to overcome.

"I bet you made a list," Jamie said suddenly, his face tight, his words emphasized as he dropped his fork, letting it clatter on to his plate.

"Jamie."

"I bet you made a fucking list about—"

"Jamie, language," his mom interrupted hurriedly. "Your sister—"

"The pros and cons of being gay," Jamie finished.

"Jamie," Daniel said softly. "Please." He'd known in his heart Jamie would be the hardest sell.

"Whatever, Daniel." Jamie's voice was flat and devoid of obvious emotion. "It's your life; s'not as if it matters to me. Though I thought we were brothers. It would have been nice to be part of the thinking process."

You were, Jamie, you were… you just didn't know it.

"Jamie."

"Whatever, dude, it's no biggie. You are what you are. Can you pass me the potatoes?" Jamie's input ended abruptly.

"That explains it then," Mark said suddenly, waving a sausage in the air on the end of his fork.

"Explains what?" Daniel said quietly, waiting for the worst. Had Mark known?

"That pink shirt you always wear. Kind of explains it now if you're gay." Then he went back to non-stop eating.

"What does gay mean?" Megan piped up.

Silence again.

"It just means Daniel is kind of special in terms of whom he'll want to love," Sue offered gently, "and he'll need our support to work it all out."

"He's always been different," Megan pointed out from her nine-year-old perspective. "He's nice to me. Not like Jamie and Mark." There, that was her input. She evidently considered enough had been said, and she too carried on with eating.

His mom cast a sympathetic look his way, intercepted by an increasingly wriggly Jamie, who just sighed.

"I got homework," Jamie said quickly. "I'm going to go up."

"Jamie, your food."

"Need to… do stuff…"

And then he left. Six feet of gangly legs and arms, tripping over himself in his haste to leave the room. Daniel felt his world tilt. He hadn't seen disgust on Jamie's face, but for his brother to leave him without looking him in the eye? That was hard.

"I promise you I won't rub people's noses in it," Daniel said softly. Disappointment sucked at him over Jamie's discomfort.

"Rub all you want," Mark said supportively. Then, realizing what he'd said, he collapsed back into his chair, giggling. Sue and Don soon joined in, and then Megan did too. She wouldn't get the joke, but Mark's laugh was infectious.

Daniel smiled at the people left at the table. He loved them all so much. It meant everything that it was no big deal.

He didn't doubt there would be issues, and when, or if, he finally got the courage up to have a boyfriend, he was convinced there would need to be discussions. Until then, he soaked in the love and acceptance of his family, pushing aside the knowledge he needed to speak to Jamie sooner rather than later.

Sue dished up bowls of ice cream, handing two with spoons to Daniel and shooing him away to find his brother, knowing the two boys needed to talk.

Daniel walked upstairs, his feet heavy and his heart anxious, until finally he stood outside Jamie's *Star Wars*-stickered door. He knocked.

As brothers, they had started knocking on each other's doors when Jamie had stumbled giggling into Mark's room to share a prank, only to discover a very embarrassed older brother flicking through girlie mags with his dick in his hand. It was a memory forever imprinted in Daniel's mind, as it had been up to him to explain to Sue why Mark was shouting and Jamie was laughing.

"Jamie," he called softly

"Go 'way." Jamie's voice sounded croaky and dry.

Daniel sighed and slumped down to rest against Jamie's door, the bowls balanced on his bent knees, the ice cream melting.

"Jamie, please, can we talk?"

"Don't wanna talk, don't need to talk."

"Jamie, I get what you're feeling."

"No you don't."

"I guess you're feeling pretty disgusted with me right now," Daniel said sadly.

Silence and then the door opened sharply, causing Daniel and both ice cream bowls to tumble into the chaos that was Jamie's room.

"What the fuck?" Jamie spat out. "What did you just say?"

"I said I kind of understand you... you probably feel a bit disgusted right now, and I can understand—"

Daniel wasn't a large or heavy guy by any means and was used to losing any and all games of wrestling that he foolishly entered into with either of his brothers. But to be dragged up to stand in front of his much taller, generally larger, boy as if he was a lightweight was a bit of a shock. And then to be pulled into a patented Jamie-hug, gripped so tight it hurt to breathe?

Well, that kind of swung the general consensus of opinion toward not disgusted.

Abruptly, Jamie pushed him away and started pacing from one dirty sock to an overflowing gym bag and back again.

"I. Am. Not. Disgusted."

"Okay," Daniel started doubtfully.

"I'm not... it's just..." Jamie stopped pacing suddenly and, with a huff, settled on the side of his bed.

"What, Jamie? Talk to me. Please." Jamie "Motor-mouth" Walker not knowing what to say was starting to scare Daniel.

"I guess I'm kind of hurt this is the first thing I've heard about the big gay switch."

"Jamie, this was something I needed to accept myself." He said it like some sort of defense. They had shared everything from reaction to first kisses to porn, from masturbation tips to kissing techniques. Daniel knew what he should have done, but his fantasies and his desires were far too wrapped in Jamie to ever begin to think of sharing his acceptance of this with him.

"I've always looked after you, looked out for you, Dan. I've stopped my geek-boy brother from being picked on. I've tried to keep you safe and stop you from going back to the dark place you were in when we were younger. I have, you know. And how am I supposed to keep you safe now?"

"Jamie."

"There are people out there, Dan, people in school, in California, outside California... Jeez... They'll want to hurt you because you're different, and I won't always be there to look after you."

"Jamie."

"I mean it Daniel, what if someone decides to beat up the different one, and failing everything else they find you?"

"Jamie, I can look after myself, I need--"

"No! You can't, Dan. You can't look after yourself, buried in your books, with your arty friends and your music, you are like a walking target as it is, Jesus Daniel, have you never noticed me running interference?"

"I have, Jamie, and I know why you do it, and I love you for it but... I'll be alone well enough soon anyway. You know with us at different colleges and whatever, and maybe I need to start standing on my own two feet without you being there. Maybe I needed to get this thing out here where I feel safe so I can... get used to it, I suppose."

"Dan... I don't want you to have to be on your own... at all." Jamie sounded heartbroken and his face was creased in misery.

"Jamie is this about me being gay, or is this about us going to different colleges?"

Jamie bent his head, picking at the dripping ice cream on his shirt, "Well shit, up until half an hour ago it was just the college thing, but now…"

Daniel moved to sit next to Jamie, shoulders touching.

"I'm sorry Jamie, I wish it was different, that I could choose what you see is the safe path, but I can't."

Jamie pushed his arm against Daniel. "You know I wouldn't have you any other way, dude. You announcing you're gay? That doesn't worry me at all. It's just, remember this is California, and please… for me… be safe, yeah?"

"I'll do everything I can to be safe Jamie."

"And you'll always use condoms?" Jamie smirked.

"Jeez, Jamie, too much." Daniel laughed, falling back on Jamie's bed, Jamie following suit, ice cream everywhere.

"Condoms, promise me."

"I need a boyfriend first."

"TMI dude, TMI."

Chapter Five

Then

FOREVER HEREAFTER KNOWN AS THE GREAT OP DESTRUCTION incident, the day that Jamie and Daniel broke Mark's heart was indelibly marked on all three of them but for very different reasons.

It was a well-thought-out plan, or rather it was if you were nine years old.

Scratch that. It was a well-thought-out plan if you were a normal nine-year-old, not nine years old and called Jamie Alexander Walker.

Daniel was the lookout, but considering this was only day two in his new house, he wasn't much of a lookout, and when Mark climbed the stairs, saw his door open, and saw a very nervous looking Daniel standing outside his room, he immediately placed Jamie in his room doing god knows what.

"Jamie."

"Mark."

"Put it down."

"Make me."

"Jamie, you little shit."

Thump, smack, jump, laugh, giggle.

Smash.

"Mom!"

Daniel was horrified and hid in his room, curled up in a tight ball on his bed, facing the wall. They were going to see it was his fault, and they were going to make him go back to the home. He didn't really want that. He liked his new family, liked his room, and his fingers felt itchy, like maybe he wanted to play the piano, which was a good sign.

Words filtered up from downstairs, and he tried not to listen.

"And what were you thinking dragging Daniel into your plans? Poor guy is up in his room scared out of his wits," Sue said. "And, Mark, you don't hit your brother, no matter what."

"But Optimus is broken." Mark was whining.

"I'm sorry, Mom." Jamie sounded sad.

"Apologize to your brother, not me."

"I'm sorry, Mark."

"And apologize to Daniel. Go upstairs and say you're sorry to him."

"Okay, Mom…"

Daniel heard the footsteps on the stairs and curled himself tighter.

"Hey, Daniel, Mom said I should 'pologize."

"Okay," Daniel muttered.

"You okay?"

"Yeah, tired."

"Okay, you goin' to bed?"

"Yeah."

"Okay."

Mark cried in the hallway because his beloved robot had been destroyed.

Jamie cried in the hallway because he was so grounded from the hoop for two weeks.

Daniel cried under his sheets because he had been shown a good place to be, and he didn't want to lose it. Not now.

Now

The first day back at school after what Jamie thought as the big reveal was a strange one.

They did the usual thing, traveling and arriving together, and then with a casual "later", they would split up.

Despite being in the same class year, they had very different friends. It wasn't a deliberate decision, but Jamie was so involved in the SA basketball team that his social life revolved around practicing, playing, strategizing, after-game pizza, and lots of flirting with the basketball babes, the cheerleaders that followed the team around.

Jamie watched Daniel cross to the other side where his friends sat, Steve with his guitar, Ella with her sketchpad, and Lewis with his laptop. Good friends, all top of their respective classes in every subject, driven, clever, and so far away from the "it" crowd it was actually quite socially acceptable to be sitting there. It helped, of course, that Daniel's brother was *the* Jamie Walker. So in general they were left alone to do whatever the popular kids thought geeks did.

Some of the cheerleaders had commented to Jamie once it was a waste that someone as pretty as Daniel was sitting way over there under the tree with the geeks and wasn't over with

Jamie and them. When Jamie looked down at teased blonde hair and red lipstick and chewing gum, he kind of wished he were sitting under the tree with Daniel. He didn't say that. He loved being captain of the basketball team. He didn't always enjoy the enforced social hierarchy that came with it and tried to avoid it most of the time, but he was aware he had a face to show to the world. It was just very hard sometimes to do that.

When Jamie reached the group of his friends, his closest friend, Tyler, the best defense player the school had ever seen, was lost in a tangle of hands and legs with Tara, the head cheerleader. Jamie could kind of make out where one finished and the other ended, but it took concentration. One of the other girls, Alex or something, spotted his arrival and made a beeline, which he couldn't avoid.

"Jamie," she said, hand on hip and the other one waggling in front of his face, "you are so in trouble with Lucy."

Lucy? Lucy? Oh shit. Prom Lucy. Wasn't he supposed to be organizing a date or something? It was just not high on his list.

"I need to find her. I'm gone," he said quickly, slapping Tyler on the back, muttering expected encouragement and slinking into the school, trying to avoid any blondes who looked remotely like Lucy, and finally finding his way to the drama department.

"Jamie, hey," Mrs. Monroe, drama teacher extraordinaire and the main reason Jamie might try majoring in drama at college. Drama didn't naturally fit with a basketball scholarship, but he was feeling quite enthused and excited at the thought. He hadn't shared his thoughts with his mom and dad, but Daniel knew. Daniel talked him through plays and scripts and helped him understand the sides of this art his analytical brain couldn't handle.

"Hey, Mrs. Monroe."

"You hiding again, Jamie?"

"S'pose so."

"Wanna help sort through these old scripts?"

Spend half hour closeted in the dust of the drama room or stand in the sunshine with his friends?

No competition.

"Where do I start?

Chapter Six

LUCY WATCHED FROM THE WINGS AS HER BOYFRIEND practiced his lines with that Ella girl. Technically Jamie wasn't her boyfriend... yet... But he would be if all went well today. She planned to corner him and talk about the prom, which despite being months away, was as good an excuse as any to drag Jamie to "planning" sessions.

She watched as Jamie said something, causing Ella to curl up, her hands on his arm, laughing to the point of tears. Lucy thought she would be jealous if it wasn't for the fact that cardigan-wearing hippy Ella was the least of her rivals in the school for Jamie's attentions. Still, she was cross Ella felt she could touch Jamie in that way and stepped forward, making herself known. Since Lucy had decided Jamie was going to be her first, she had been stalking him relentlessly. She knew his timetable, his address, his cell phone number, his shoe size, his eye color, his basketball stats... everything. It was a military operation she and her girlfriends had dubbed the "getting into Jamie's pants" plan.

He was so gorgeous. Tall, blond, confident, and with the

most stunning blue eyes. Top that with he was captain of a team and that made him king as far as she was concerned.

"Jamie," she called in her best laughing isn't-this-a-coincidence-to-see-you-here voice. He turned, surprise and a small amount of embarrassment on his face.

"Hey, Lucy," he said, turning to Ella and saying something low before jumping down off the stage with a cat's grace and standing tall next to her.

"Jamie, we really need to start thinking about prom, I need to pin you down for a chat."

"Okay, yeah, I've been meaning to catch up with you, sorry."

"No worries. How 'bout Saturday? My parents are away this weekend, and I thought we could have the first committee meeting at my house."

"Sounds cool. What time?"

"Seven."

"I'll be there."

When he turned to climb back up on stage, his tight ass clearly visible in his jeans, it was all Lucy could do not to drool. This Saturday, he was all hers.

DANIEL HAD OBSERVED the exchange from the side of the stage where he sat with Steve, humming along to his guitar, lost in planning music for the latest show. He had watched carefully as Lucy Simmonds had simpered and smirked around his brother, running manicured nails across Jamie's bare arm, seeing his brother's answering smile and relaxed stance.

So far Jamie had managed nothing but short-term flings,

and Daniel knew for certain none of them, despite Jamie's reputation, had gone past third base. Mark teased him for it, Daniel silently thanked him for it, but at the end of the day, Jamie, at sixteen, wasn't like a typical sixteen-year-old boy and had evidently waited until seventeen to finally get with the program. Mark despaired.

"You're the basketball captain; you're bright, good-looking-ish. You could have any girl you want. What is the matter with you?"

"They're just boring, man, and all they do is shop and talk crap about shoes and stuff."

"So stop them talking. Jeez, do I need to draw diagrams?"

Jamie had been stubborn in his resolve. He wasn't waiting for marriage, or long-term, he just wanted his first time to have meaning, to be what he wanted, and most of all, it would be nice if he was sober when it happened. Mark huffed, left new porn mags on his brother's bed, and told him wild stories of college life. None of it worked. Jamie was not changing his mind.

So as Daniel watched this Lucy girl touching and flirting, he hoped this wasn't the girl that gave his brother meaning in his life, hoped he wouldn't hand himself over on a plate for meaningless sex just because Mark told him to.

He wanted Jamie to wait for the one. And in his wildest imaginings that one would be him. He sighed. Fighting this attraction to freaking Jamie was killing him.

It wasn't as if Daniel would ever have Jamie anyway. This one-sided attraction would forever remain that way. Jamie would go to college, meet some girl, preferably not skanky Lucy, have a lot of heterosexual no-ties sex, fall in love or get married someday.

He never spent much time analyzing his attraction for

Jamie. He just knew it was there and had been for a few years, ever since he realized he was fantasizing about Jamie's hands, arms, legs, ass, eyes, hair… and not about the girls in the porn mags he had grabbed from Mark's stash.

He would never even dream of doing anything about it. Jamie was his foster-brother, the other half of him, and college would give him the breathing room he needed to find a partner and forget the love he felt for his best friend as well as he could. It was self-preservation that made Daniel choose different colleges from Jamie. If they went to the same one, and Daniel was exposed to the heartbreak of seeing Jamie happy with someone else… shit, it wasn't worth thinking about.

Then

He didn't come out of his bedroom for dinner. He was a little bit scared and a lot worried that his part in the destruction of Mark's prize toy would be a big thing. As big a thing as when Daniel got scruffy and dirty playing with the neighbors' dog when he was seven, just as his mom and dad were hosting a party thing in their house. They were both horrified and embarrassed, and the tears that fell down his face that night had been hot and scorching.

He didn't want that again; it had made him feel small and sad.

"Daniel." That was Sue's voice at his door, and he felt the mattress dip as she sat on the side of his *bed*. She lay back against the headboard, her hands soft in his long hair. "Are you okay, sweetie?"

"M'okay," Daniel replied, his breath hitching and his eyes raw with holding back more tears.

"Honey, I know this is all overwhelming for you. It doesn't help you've landed in a family as boisterous as ours. I just want you to know that, at this moment, Mark and Jamie are on the Nintendo, desperate for you to come down and see the new game they have." She paused, waiting for that to sink in, smiling softly as Daniel moved his thin body round to face her.

"They… they don't hate each other?" he said, wondering, his face creased in confusion.

"No, Dan, they could never hate each other. Of course Mark is hurt that Jamie chose his dearest possession in the world to use for a prank; Jamie is hurt because we all see he did it to score marks with you, and now he feels embarrassed and ashamed at his stupidity."

Daniel knew all about embarrassed and ashamed. Poor Jamie. "So it's okay?"

"Of course. Their dad and I have spoken our bit, Jamie has promised to buy Mark a new one, Mark has also exacted punishment on Jamie and is making him do the dishes for two weeks, which is normally Mark's chore. It's all handled."

"What about me? Is Mark angry with me? He should be; I was just as involved. I deserve punishment as well."

"No, Daniel, he knows what his little brother is like, knows you were just pulled along for the ride."

"Oh." Daniel felt oddly disappointed he was being left out of the punishment. He didn't want to be a special case.

"But, Daniel, I think it would go some way to making Mark see you are sorry if you were to do the dishes with Jamie."

"Really?"

"Yes, really. Now, why don't you freshen up and come

downstairs and watch this battle thing the boys have? It'll be time for dinner soon."

"I will."

And then Sue left, leaving a very happy Daniel lying back on his bed, a tiny, very tiny, feeling of belonging starting to grow inside.

Chapter Seven

Now

IT WAS ABOUT SIX ON SATURDAY NIGHT BEFORE JAMIE remembered the whole prom thing at Lucy's house, half way through a game of one-on-one with Daniel, which caused him to hesitate, meaning Daniel actually managed to shoot a hoop. He followed up with his dorky "I've beaten Jamie" dance, which involved much jumping and flailing of hands.

Jamie flopped down on the grass. "Dork," he said affectionately. Daniel slid to the ground next to him.

"Twelve-One, Twelve-One," he singsonged, and pushed Jamie's arm.

"I was distracted. I've just remembered I've got this Lucy prom thing at seven."

"Plenty of time to make yourself pretty, man," Daniel offered helpfully. Jamie snorted and rolled over on his stomach, his T-shirt catching and moving up, his shorts riding low.

"Dan, I really don't want this whole prom thing, dude."

"You won't have to do much, just look pretty!" Daniel snarked.

"Ass," Jamie retorted, thumping Daniel's arm. "I mean I'm not even sure I wanna go to the prom. It's just this whole load of have and have-not bullshit, ya know?"

"Jeez, Jamie, that almost sounded deep."

"Ha ha," Jamie deadpanned. "No. I'm serious. I mean it's not going to be acceptable for me to stand with you. I'll have to do that whole cool jock thing, and you'll be doing your whole geeky thing on the opposite side of the room, and it'll be no fun at all."

"Jamie, how the fuck are you going to cope on a basketball scholarship, dude? You are going to be a full-time jock then."

Jamie plucked at the grass in front of him, then he sighed and rested his head on crossed hands, turning to face Daniel, their faces only inches apart, so close that Jamie could see every fleck of silver and dark gray in Daniel's expressive eyes.

"I've been thinking about that. I had a letter this morning, and I kind of got accepted into the UCLA arts program for drama."

"No shit." Daniel sounded shocked, and Jamie couldn't look him in the eyes. Daniel was right to be shocked. What kind of idiot gave up a scholarship to try his hand at acting?

"Mrs. Monroe put in a letter of recommendation, and I got the place if I want it. I mean it isn't fully funded, no scholarship, but I spoke to Mom, and she has the money from Gran's trust for me to go, the same way she funds Mark at college."

"Jamie, that is big. Huge."

"Very big, I don't want my life defined by basketball. I want to be something different; I wanna act, go on stage, maybe direct, I dunno. I just know I don't want to pretend anymore."

"Jamie—"

"It was you."

"Me?"

"Coming out and telling us, and being so brave, and starting a whole new life as you. Not pretending to be something you couldn't be. Having no secrets from us. I admire that, Dan, and I want to have that too."

"What secrets could you possibly have, Jamie?" Daniel had laughter in his voice, and for the first time ever, how Daniel was reacting was hurting him.

Jamie paused, shutting his eyes, the sun shining down on his back. When he opened his eyes again, he said, "I suppose I'm a geek stuck in a jock's body, if that makes sense."

"Okay" was all Daniel said.

"Moron," Jamie replied.

"Ass."

Jamie couldn't think of a comeback on that one. He failed big time.

LUCY ANSWERED THE DOOR, dressed in what Jamie loosely described as "not very much". Short shorts, short T-shirt, and hair artfully teased and tousled about her thin shoulders.

"Hey, Jamie," she said in that annoyingly, grating, singsong voice he supposed was her attempt at flirting. "Come on in."

He followed her into the front room, sitting on the sofa, taking in the house around him, its grandeur, its opulence, its freaking great TV. Mark would have been stoked to see that.

"Sorry I'm late," he apologized. He hadn't been that late, only fifteen minutes, but he hated letting people down.

"That's okay."

"Where is everyone?" Jamie asked a bit nervous, not seeing evidence of anyone else in the house. He winced as Lucy sat down next to him, her scarlet-tipped fingers resting on his thigh.

"S'just you and me tonight, Jamie. Thought we could start the ball rolling on our own, y'know, just the two of us?"

"Erm…"

Shit.

DANIEL SAT bolt upright as six feet of Walker leaped on his bed.

"What the fuck?" he said. Removing his earphones, he tried to still his scared-to-death heart.

"Dude? Were you asleep?" Jamie asked.

"Resting my eyes."

"It's nine on a Saturday. Shouldn't you be out finding a nice piece of ass?"

"Jamie."

"Sorry. Shit, Dan, I have had the worst night."

"With the prom group?"

"Try the prom couple; it was just me and Lucy."

"Oh."

"Yes, oh. She answered the door in this…" He flailed his arm around indicating clothes. "Well, in practically nothing, and then told me tonight was a private session just for her and me."

"I'm following it so far, and the problem with that is?"

"Dude, ewwww, this is Lucy."

"Yeah, *the* Lucy, the girl every boy in the school is after, well, apart from me." Daniel smirked

"She made it quite clear that she and I… that we… that shit, Dan, no."

"You don't wanna do the wild thing with Lucy I'm-fantastic Simmonds?"

"No way, like I said, ewww."

"And you are on my bed because?"

"I need help, man, help and advice, and… shit."

"You want heterosexual relationship advice from the gay guy?"

"No, I wanna plot how I get out of Lucy's evil clutches with my best plan maker."

"Just tell her," Daniel offered.

"Call that a plan?"

"Erm… yeah?"

"You are shit at plan making."

"Uh-huh, says the boy who orchestrated the whole Optimus Prime debacle."

"Are you ever going to let me forget that?"

"Nope."

FINALLY IN BED, Daniel lay on his back, staring at some distant point on his ceiling, thinking back over the day. The news they might be going to the same college after all, the whole Lucy thing, Jamie's admission about not being bothered to attend prom when he was a shoo-in for prom king?

It was all too much.

And when they lay in the sun talking and Jamie's T-shirt

had ridden up to reveal a tantalizing strip of skin? God, it had been so hard to cover his blatant staring.

Added to that they had sat squashed next to each other on the bed for hours plotting and planning, and Daniel couldn't handle the proximity for much longer. Every fantasy he had. Every thought he had. Everything seemed to center round Jamie, and it was on the tip of his tongue to actually tell him.

To tell him, though, meant losing everything, losing a family—losing *his* family. He wasn't prepared to do that.

He needed to calm the hell down and keep his fantasies where they belonged, between him and his right hand.

———

JAMIE'S MIND flew over the cringing experience that was Lucy.

Perhaps he should just tell her.

Perhaps he should be honest.

Perhaps he should just say, I don't fancy you, I don't fancy anyone, I just wanna spend time with Daniel.

Just with Daniel.

Chapter Eight

THEY WERE FIVE GAMES INTO THE NEW SEASON, AND JAMIE was feeling every day of his seventeen years. Every muscle ached, and he felt like he was dragging around a body made of lead.

"You look sick, dude," one of his teammates offered helpfully, but he refused to sit this one out, regretting it only after they had won with a close result. He remembered sitting down on the bench, he remember being handed the bottle of water, he even remembered trying to drink it, his head pounding, his hands shaking and his chest tight.

There was a lot of talking around him, lots of buzzing irritating noise, and then a familiar voice.

"Jamie… Jamie, we need to get you home. You look like shit."

"Dan," he said, but his voice was croaky and dry. He focused on Daniel as he was helped to his feet and taken out through the back entrance to the cars, his mom fussing, his dad organizing, and Daniel just holding him upright.

He slunk into the backseat of the car, feeling his mom touching his head.

"He's burning hot," she said softly

"I knew something wasn't right during the game." His dad's voice.

"We should have pulled him out."

"He's a responsible boy, Sue; he can make his own decisions."

Finally he heard Daniel's voice, soft and persuasive. "Let's just get him home to bed." He climbed in next to Jamie and pulled him close to him in a brotherly hug, leaning back and tucking him under his neck and letting him lay on his chest. He felt so cold, but he was sweating, his skin burning against Daniel's face. Daniel used his free hand to rub soothing circles into Jamie's back, holding him as Jamie coughed sharply and winced at the pain in his chest.

"I suppose…," their mom started conversationally. "It was kind of inevitable he caught Megan's bug."

"Well, at least he'll be happy they won the game," their dad said.

Jamie just let their voices roll over him, instead snuggling closer to Daniel. He shifted against him, a free hand coming up to curl in Daniel's shirt.

He's my brother, he's my best friend, and I feel so ill.

They made the drive home in record time, and Jamie swallowed painkillers then allowed Daniel to help him into bed. Jamie vaguely realized Daniel had pulled in the airbed and his quilt. Ever since the being-sick-in-quiet incident, whenever one of the two of them was ill the other would sleep on the floor in the sick room. Their mom had tried to discourage it, but at the end of the day, it was a losing battle against the combined front of the sons she called her terrible twins.

Jamie immediately turned over in bed, groaning and clutching at his pillow, coughing pathetically. Daniel and his mom exchanged wry smiles; Jamie just closed his eyes. He knew he wasn't a good patient at the best of times, kind of wimpy and moaning and miserable, but Daniel was used to him. They looked after each other when one of them was ill. It all stemmed back to the summer after he had arrived at the Walkers and his first real ever fever.

Then

Daniel had been feeling sick all day. At first he put it down to the fact that Jamie had opened his lips while eating his burger and showed his grossed-out siblings the contents of his mouth. Because that right there? That was when he started to feel really sick. That had been the night before.

It got worse the next day. In school, by first break, he had pains in his side and could feel sweat on his back. The teacher commented that he looked very pale, but Daniel dismissed the concern as just feeling hot. Given it was a very warm Cali summer's day, no one could dispute that fact.

By lunchtime, he was almost doubled over in pain, standing over the toilet and losing his breakfast in spectacular fashion, feeling very dizzy and falling head first into the side of the cubicle.

"Daniel, Dan."

Go away, m'tired, sore

"Daniel, darling, can you wake up for me?"

Sue's voice, then another, younger, in tears. Jamie.

"He didn't say anything mom; he just hid in the toilets, I don't get it why he didn't…"

"Daniel, open your eyes."

"Daniel."

When his eyes opened for the first time, it was to the view of a ceiling and an awful lot of white. He felt a cool hand on his forehead.

"Dan, honey, we were worried." Sue's voice.

Daniel knew what he needed to say. He needed to say anything that meant he wasn't going to be fostered elsewhere.

"M'sorry," he mumbled, as close to what he felt in his heart as he could find. He didn't want to be an inconvenience, always tried his hardest to not cause a ripple in the house.

"Don't be sorry, sweetie. It was your appendix, nothing you did, nothing could have stopped it."

"Still sorry… for worry," he whispered, his mouth dry.

"I'm going to take Jamie home now, sweetie. I'll be back in an hour."

"Don't," Daniel whispered the word forced from him in a rush of air.

"Don't what, honey?"

"Don't leave me here."

"Only for a few hours, just to get Megan—"

"Not on my own."

"I'll stay." This came from Jamie, who really sounded like he was crying.

"Jamie honey."

"I want to stay. I don't want Daniel to be frightened," he said with all the ten-year-old solemnity he could manage.

"I'll be gone an hour. Is that okay with you, Daniel, if Jamie stays?"

"Please."

"Okay, I'll tell them at the desk. Stay in the room and no wandering about."

"I won't," Jamie agreed immediately, and then sat himself on the side of the bed, his arms and legs crossed Indian style, looking for all the world like a responsible little adult.

When Sue left and during the in-between time before sleep claimed him, Jamie asked Daniel one question. "Why didn't you want to be alone, Dan?"

"Didn't want you to leave me and never come back for me, 'cause you don't want me anymore."

To this day, Daniel wasn't sure if he ever actually said that out loud or said it just in his dreams. Jamie never said anything, and Daniel never thought it again, especially when Sue bustled back in the room and fell asleep in the chair next to his bed, an exhausted long-limbed Jamie in her arms, proving she still wanted to be with him, that he was worth the worry.

Now

"Dan."

Daniel woke immediately, rolling awkwardly on the airbed and thumping his head on the nightstand with a muffled ouch.

"You okay?" he asked worriedly, feeling his head. "Do you want me to get Mom?"

"Nah, I'm good, just need some more painkillers for my freakin' head and some water."

"Is your head bad?"

"Like hammers, dude."

Daniel passed him the tablets and the water, helping him to coordinate taking them, until Jamie lay back shaky and exhausted to the pillows.

"You on the floor?" Jamie croaked, his voice low.

"Yeah."

Jamie rolled to his side and scooted across his double bed,

leaving space for Dan. "You're going to get the virus anyway, Dan, get in."

So Daniel, against his better judgment, crawled on top of the covers, Jamie radiating warmth, and lay back waiting until Jamie's breathing slowed to soft and settled.

He moved to his side, looking at Jamie, at his lashes fanning his high cheekbones, his short hair sweat slicked to his head, his tanned skin, so the opposite of Daniel's fair skin. He just looked.

Then, sure that Jamie was asleep, he dropped a small kiss to Jamie's hot forehead, whispering his love for his brother onto damp skin and then fell back to the pillow, sleep claiming him quickly.

Jamie had been right.

Three days later, it became obvious he had caught the virus.

And Jamie crawled into his bed with him, fed him painkillers, and helped him drink water.

That was what they did.

Chapter Nine

CHRISTMAS WAS QUIET, JUST THE SIX OF THEM. DANIEL loved every minute of it, so different from Thanksgiving where the world descended on them.

They played games.

Daniel and Jamie annoyed Mark, Mark teased Megan, and Don and Sue spent a lot of time in the kitchen alone "cooking".

All in all, the perfect day.

Daniel had access to money, a lot of money, basically a substantial trust fund from various life insurances. He didn't touch a penny of it for gifts. Every gift he gave was bought from money he had earned for Christmas by shelf stacking at the supermarket, and the present giving was that much more satisfying for it.

Jamie and Dan snuck beer up to Daniel's room when Megan had gone to bed and Mark had gone to visit his girlfriend's family. It ended up as it always did, the two of them sitting on the bed, backs against the wall, chatting.

Jamie revealed he had another Christmas present for Daniel, who eagerly ripped off the paper.

"Porn? You got me a skin mag?"

"Not just any skin mag, dude." Jamie leaned over smelling of Christmas dinner and new aftershave. "It's a gay skin mag."

Daniel blushed as Jamie flicked through, stopping at a page showing two men doing… stuff.

"Jeez, that is actually quite hot," Jamie said on a soft breath. "I could get into that whole being pushed around bit."

"Dude," Daniel snapped, shutting the mag and sliding it under his pillow.

"Well, like with a girl, it's all soft and, well, gentle and stuff, but two dudes… Can you imagine, hard and strong? It could be a real battle for like who takes the lead."

"Uh huh." Daniel really didn't want this conversation with the object of his lustful thoughts sitting next to him, but his traitorous dick was getting other ideas. He shifted uncomfortably and began looking to change the subject, but Jamie just wouldn't let it lie.

"You've kissed girls. Did it really do nothing for you at all?"

"Not really."

"So how long have you—"

"Jamie."

"Hey, enquiring minds want to know."

"You mean nosey minds."

"Nuh-uh, we share everything."

Not everything, Daniel thought to himself and blushed again. "Yeah," he said softly.

"So have you kissed a dude yet?"

Daniel's head shot up. "No, Jamie."

"Then—" Jamie flapped his hand a bit. "—how do you know you're gay?"

"It isn't that easy, Jamie. It's not all about kissing and shit.

It's inside of you, part of you, you just know."

"Yeah, so let's do it."

"Do what."

"Kiss."

"What the fuck?"

"It's what we do, right? We do everything together. We can see, yeah?"

"See what?" Daniel asked curiously, not sure where this was going.

"See if the feelings I have in me means I could like what you like."

"What feelings?"

"Shit, I don't know. I know I don't want you out of my sight. Maybe it's jealousy that you know what you are, know your own mind. Maybe I want that. But I also have something inside of me that feels like ants under my skin, and I just don't understand it." Jamie sounded stressed and agitated. "Hell, I don't know how I feel about anything. But I looked at this magazine and I felt… stuff."

"Jamie—"

"No, Dan, I'm serious, I don't know what it feels like, I could never know my own mind like you, but I just feel so damn confused at what you're telling me you are."

"Kissing me won't make that go away, Jamie," Dan said sadly. He would do anything for Jamie, but this seemed to be pushing it too far even for them.

"Just one kiss," Jamie cajoled. "You've never kissed a guy, and I want to know what it's like. C'mon."

Shit. The eyes. The damn puppy eyes and that damn spiky hair.

"One kiss, no tongues."

"Okay."

They turned to each other. Awkward. Daniel's dick hard

and leaking and hidden in loose sweats.

This is so wrong; I'm going to hell.

This is so hot, shit, I never thought.

Jamie moved closer, running the tip of his tongue over dry lips. Daniel unconsciously followed the movement, wanting to take his own hand and palm his dick but resisting the urge so strong it made him sweat.

"What now?" Daniel said, just for something to fill the silence. Jamie coughed and leaned in. Daniel leaned in, pulled by an invisible force.

Their lips met. Jamie angled his head instinctively, and Daniel moved one of his traitorous hands to touch Jamie's shoulder as the pressure became more and the kiss became harder. Jamie breathed, his tongue brushing the corner of Daniel's lips, and a leap of lightning went straight to his dick. Daniel opened his mouth slightly. He was kissing Jamie, his tongue touched Jamie's, his tongue twisted with Jamie's. His head fell to one side, a better angle. *Oh my God.*

They pulled apart at the same moment, eyes open and caught in each other's gaze.

"Fuck," Jamie said softly. "That was the hottest fucking kiss I have ever—"

And then Daniel pulled him in for another kiss, feeling Jamie lean in at first and then abruptly pull back.

"One kiss, dude." Jamie laughed, an embarrassed tone to his voice, scrambling back and standing. "'Night, Dan," he said hurriedly and backed out of the room, pulling the door closed behind him.

Daniel followed him to the door and locked it, falling back on his bed, his hand going straight to his dick, pulling once, twice, a third time and coming over his fingers, the orgasm explosive.

"Shit, fuck, shit."

Chapter Ten

HIS FACE FLAMING, AND HIS DICK HARD AND LEAKING, JAMIE had his hands already there as he stumbled into his own room, closing the door and sinking to his knees. On a gasp, he was coming hot and heavy over his own hand, the taste of Daniel in his mouth, Daniel's eyes, full of lust and hurt and confusion, burning into his brain.

Just to touch Daniel, just to taste him, blew his mind. Soft kissable lips, hard pressure, and, jeez, that tongue, searching and pushing and tasting. And God.

Jamie hit his head back on the door, once, twice, three times. Why the fuck had he done that? Why push Daniel? Why hurt Daniel that way? He was used to taking things too far. He was Jamie Walker, that is what he did, and Daniel went with most of the usual crap Jamie threw his way. But this time, he had out-Jamied himself in spectacular fashion. How the hell was he going to explain the fact he had just had one of the most intense orgasms since he'd found his right hand and the magic it created when used on his dick?

He wasn't gay.

Daniel was gay, though, damn it.

He banged his head back again, connecting with the door in a painful crack.

He wasn't gay. He loved his brother. It had been an experiment. Everyone did stuff like that.

He just needed to go find a girl to counteract the obvious gayness of what he had just done.

That would fix it.

And if he couldn't get Daniel's eyes—the depth of gray, the pure emotion—out of his head then surely that was only a post-orgasmic image ingrained on his retinas, similar to Miss July and her sprawled classic car pose.

He reached up, locked the door, then crawled on hands and knees to his bed, cleaning himself up and climbing under the covers. He forced his eyes closed, willing sleep, willing no dreams.

DANIEL FELL INTO A FITFUL SLEEP, full of Jamie and touch and kisses, and it was only an hour later that he jolted awake, just at the point Jamie was closing in for another kiss in the latest of his heated, sleep-heavy thought processes.

Moaning in frustration, he climbed off the bed. Maybe a hot drink would help.

Once he reached the kitchen, he boiled water in the kettle and rummaged for the hot chocolate, finally finding it and placing it next to the mug.

"Can I have one?"

Daniel jumped two foot in the air before twisting to face the owner of the voice. "Jeez, Meg, you scared the crap outta me."

"Can I have one?"

"What you doing up, squirt?" he asked gently, ruffling her

hair with one hand, which she batted away with a tired sleepy smile.

"Couldn't sleep," she said. "Heard you come downstairs, so I followed ya."

"Go sit on the sofa, I'll bring it in."

"M'ok."

Daniel made the hot drinks, adding extra milk to Megan's cup, and carried them through to the front room, sitting next to her. He handed her the milky drink and settled back in the corner of the sofa. Instinctively she curled into his side. It was always this way; she always naturally cuddled up with Daniel, always chose him for attention over her brothers. Daniel called it love and affection. Jamie said it was more self-preservation as, in Megan's words, Daniel was nice to her, unlike her smelly pranking brothers.

He slipped an arm around her, aware he probably only had a few more years of this easy affection from her. She was ten going on fifteen. Already into boys, clothes, makeup, her age of innocence and love of dolls was well past; she was far too young for that in Daniel's opinion.

"Why can't you sleep, Meggy?"

"Was worried about stuff."

"What kind of stuff, babe?"

"I can't say."

"You can tell me."

"I can't Daniel, s'about you."

"About me?" Shit, had she been researching gay? Jesus, if she'd seen any porn.

"Yeah, 'bout 'doption."

"Adoption?" Well, that was out of left field.

"Well, you're my foster brother, right? Mom says you were only meant to stay a few months and, like, you are still here. And you could go; you're nearly eighteen. You could just go, and you wouldn't be my foster-brother any more. You wouldn't be my anything anymore."

"Megs, I would; I will always be your brother, no matter what."

"I read about adoption, and mom and dad never adopted you."

"No, Megs, they didn't." It wasn't for want of trying on their part though. "We don't need a piece of paper to say you are my sister."

"That makes me sad, 'cause you could go."

Daniel pulled Megan closer. In his heart, she was his sister, which would never change.

"They did ask me, you know. Don't think they didn't," Daniel said.

"Asked you?"

Daniel nodded. "Your mom and dad, they asked me, after a few years, I think I was twelve or so. They wanted to do the whole adoption thing, make it legal."

"Really?"

"Really."

Then

"Daniel, can we have a chat with you?"

He turned to Sue and Don, immediate guilt flushing his body. He didn't remember doing anything wrong, but hanging around with Jamie, who knew? Jamie and he exchanged guilty looks. Normally they got into trouble together, and being separated was new.

"Did he do something, 'cause it was really prolly me?"

Jamie said worriedly, moving slightly to stand in front of Daniel.

Their mom smiled. "He's not in any trouble, sweetheart. Your dad and I just need a word."

"Okay." Jamie still sounded worried, but after exchanging a look of solidarity with Daniel, he left the room and followed Mark out into the garden.

"Can you come into the study, Daniel?"

"Yes, ma'am."

In the study, Don was sitting on his sofa. Not behind his desk where he sat when he was telling the boys off, but on his cozy sofa, where he sat when he was reading to the boys or helping them with homework.

Sue indicated he should sit next to Don and then knelt in front of him on the floor.

"Don and I have been talking, and you've been fostered with us a while now, Dan…"

Daniel nodded, and his heart flipped. He knew where this was going. He'd been waiting for it nearly every day he'd been here.

"Uh-huh," he said softly, tears already pushing their way up and out, stopping only at the back of his eyes.

"Well, we'd like to make it more permanent, adopt you as one of our own," she said softly.

Daniel was startled. He hadn't been expecting that.

"It's important to us that we talk about this with you, Daniel."

"Would it mean I wouldn't be Keyes? I would be Daniel Walker?"

"Not if you didn't want to, sweetheart. This would just be our way of you knowing that you would be with us, as part of our family forever."

"Would it be different if I wasn't adopted? Could you send me away when you wanted?" That was a vital question.

Sue looked aghast. "Daniel, we would never send you away. You are as much part of this family as Jamie, Mark and Megan. Is that what you think we could do? Would do?"

Daniel was uncertain, and he didn't say anything, just shrugged.

"We want you to be our son, Daniel," Don said softly.

"Can I not be that without the whole adoption thing?" Daniel asked quietly, his teeth worrying his lower lip.

What if they wanted him to go one day? They were too special to be weighed down with him as a son. Adoption would make it a much more difficult thing for them to part company if they needed to.

He'd thought his parents were forever, and he had been proved wrong.

If the Walkers adopted him, made it permanent, then what if something happened to them too?

"Is that what you want, Daniel? To just stay with us fostered?"

Daniel raised wet eyes to the people he was thinking of as his parents; he wasn't ready for permanent. Permanent that could be taken from him by hospitals or drugs. He just wanted safe.

"Is that okay?" he asked softly, his voice wet with tears.

Sue pulled him in for a hug, and he felt Don pat his back.

"Of course it's okay, sweetheart. We want to do whatever makes you feel safe."

Daniel blinked. How did she know he wanted that? Had she read his mind? "Can I just say… would it be okay if…"

"What is it, sweetheart?"

"Is it okay if I call you and Don Mom and Dad?"

Now

"So why didn't they ask you again?" Megan said softly.

"They did. Every year they asked, and every year I found another reason why it was better for you all to have an out where I was concerned."

Megan looked up at him. She clearly didn't really understand. How could Daniel make her understand?

"It's like… I always thought it was my fault that my dad died, that it was somehow my fault my mom decided to take her own life, that I wasn't good enough for anyone to stay. I mean everyone always said I should make them proud, and I did try, but to lose parents so young kind of mucks your head up. I just always saw myself as the problem." Daniel thought back to every year they had asked him, every year he had said he was happy for it to stay as it was, and he felt the familiar sadness rise in him that he had been too scared, too much of a coward to actually ever consider saying yes.

Megan stared at him with blue eyes, so similar to Jamie's, wise beyond her years, snuggling in under Daniel's arm.

"Doesn't matter anyway," Megan said philosophically.

"Why's that, squirt?"

"I love you, Dan."

"I love you too, Megs."

"I reckon Jamie loves you too."

"I know he does."

"Not sure about Mark though."

And then they laughed. Peace.

DANIEL WOKE up the next morning his eyes gritty, his back sore from falling asleep on the sofa after Megan went back to bed. It had been five in the morning before he finally made his way back to his own bed, pausing briefly outside Jamie's door but not really knowing why.

All too soon Jamie would be up, looking at Daniel with knowing eyes, wondering why Daniel was still here.

The guilt that Daniel was feeling was all consuming.

Jamie had pulled back from a second kiss. He had done his experimentation, had pronounced the kiss as hot, and then, damn it, Daniel had leaned in for more.

More.

Shit. Daniel was suffused with a head-to-toe blush, and he leaned back on his wall, sliding down. Knees up, he wrapped his arms around them, his head resting on them, hot tears at the back of his eyes.

This wasn't harmless messing around at all.

This was breaking his heart.

Chapter Eleven

JAMIE WOKE WITH A FULL-ON HEADACHE, KNOWING IT WAS because of a lack of sleep. What had happened the night before, the whole kissing thing, the whole overhearing what Daniel was telling Megan thing. They hadn't known he was sitting on the stairs. Neither of them heard Jamie move back away from the door and climb the stairs back to his room, a frown on his face and a hand on his chest because he couldn't breathe.

He'd never really known the real reason for Daniel refusing adoption. He'd just accepted it with the understanding of youth. What he had heard just made him feel so sad, and it left him uncomfortable in his own skin. Unsettled and angsty.

To Jamie, Daniel had seemed such a vulnerable person; he always had been. Jamie had spent the last eight years looking out for him, being his brother, but had he actually ever made him feel safe? Jamie was always pulling Daniel into pranks where trouble often ensued. Was that a good thing for Daniel? Had it just made him nervous he'd get in trouble and be thrown out? Did he expect it? Did Daniel really think one day his new mom and dad would turn round to him and tell him to go? Or worse leave him?

He stood and stretched, determined he would talk to Daniel this morning and make him see he was a real part of the family.

No trial kissing, no giving into these feelings surfacing from god knows where, no more. Just working on making Daniel feel valued.

Starting now.

A knock on his door and Jamie opened it to reveal a blushing Daniel.

"We kind of need to talk," he started softly, and slipped into the room past Jamie, pushing the door shut behind him.

"We do?" Jamie replied, still blown away that Daniel was actually able to talk to him at all.

"Jamie, what happened last night…" He stopped, stricken eyes focusing on Jamie, hands nervously wringing in front of him.

Jamie didn't know what to say, half of him so desperate to touch and kiss the man in front of him, half of him fearful Daniel would say no more touching. He stared into a determined gray gaze, knowing his own eyes must be showing his nerves, his indecision.

"I want to say sorry," Daniel started nervously before Jamie could get his words out. Wait? Daniel was sorry?

"Sorry? What for? It was my idea."

"Jamie, it may have been your idea…" He paused, dropping his gaze. "I wanted to, Jamie, desperately. I wanted to kiss you. I've been fighting these really intense feelings for months now. I've focused on you so much, and I know it is wrong, and I just wanted to say how sorry I am, and please, can we forget last night? I'll try my hardest…" His breath hitched on a sob.

Jamie extended a hand in support. Daniel raised his gaze again to Jamie's. Jamie hoped he wouldn't see hate there, but what he did see moved him swiftly back against the wall.

Fire. He saw banked fire, passion, not disgust, but raw naked fire, then Jamie moved. "You don't get it, do you, Daniel? You don't see for one minute that what you feel could be two-sided? I may be confused about a lot at the moment, but when we kissed last night… that was real, that was raw." And then, leaning his whole frame against a trembling, shocked Daniel, he took control, searched for warm soft lips, and took all he could from Daniel, swallowing groans and murmurs, holding his face in two hands, heads tilting, bodies moving closer, both so damn hard.

Daniel pulled back. "Jamie, you don't want…"

"Shut up, Daniel, stop fucking thinking," Jamie growled into Daniel's open and kiss-swollen mouth, pushing his tongue in, using every ounce of his girl practice on making this the best kiss Daniel would ever have.

They pushed, they pulled, they rutted like the two horny teenagers they were, the pressure of swollen dicks on hard thighs enough to send Daniel toppling over the edge, his body tensing. Jamie followed soon after, hands gripping Daniel's hips, wringing the last drop of feeling from them both.

Then moving his lips, gentling his breathing, focusing on kissing Daniel, showing him there was hope, there could be a future for this.

And that, after it all, this was deadly fucking serious.

Jamie finally stepped back after a last gentle kiss to bruised lips, a last fleeting touch to heated skin. He expected a smack, even going so far as to flinch as he opened his eyes and stared into gray. He wanted a smile, he needed something, some gut reaction, hoping for…

Daniel's eyes filled almost immediately, and his legs just

folded under him as soon as Jamie let him go. He slumped down against the wall, his legs drawn up, his arms wrapped round them, his eyes locked on Jamie's as Jamie fell to his knees in front of him.

"What did we do?" Daniel whispered brokenly, tears tracking down his pale skin and running off his chin, "Jamie what did we do?"

Jamie placed both hands on Daniel's knees, moving in closer, tears in his own eyes, filled with confusion. "I don't know what to say," Jamie said softly. "Dan, you are starting to worry me. What is wrong?"

"That was… this isn't…" Daniel couldn't get anything past his obvious distress, his breath hitching. "I don't want…" He dropped his forehead to his bent knees; tears, so many tears.

"You don't want? You don't want this? You don't want me? What, Daniel? Talk to me." Jamie was starting to feel panic curling in his stomach. What had just happened between them was magic, had been magic, and now… Now it was just turning to ashes in his mouth.

"I can't," Daniel said brokenly, lifting his head and staring straight at Jamie. "We can't… we can't do this, Jamie."

"Daniel—"

"This is really, really…" Abruptly Daniel clambered up, using the wall for support, knocking Jamie back on his butt in the process. Blindly he pulled at the door.

Shit.

The door hadn't even been locked.

"No more, Jamie, no more," he threw over his shoulder, stumbling across the hall to his own room.

He left Jamie sitting dazed on the floor, wondering how it had all gone to hell so quickly, listening as Daniel's door locked, and he was left sitting on his own.

Then

The piano was the elephant in the room until Christmas Eve that first year Daniel had found a home with the Walkers.

They apparently always opened one present to each other on Christmas Eve. Jamie received a new action figure for his burgeoning Star Wars collection, Mark a book, Megan chocolates, Don a joke reindeer tie, Sue a chef's hat. When it came to Daniel's present, Jamie immediately jumped up and dug around for a flat parcel, muttering to himself and then pushing it toward Daniel to open. Sue looked at her middle child fondly. He was visibly vibrating with the excitement of the gift he had ordered for Daniel, with Mark's help, from Amazon.

Daniel nervously pulled at the paper. He had had Christmases before. He hadn't been deprived, but his Christmases had consisted of gifts at a restaurant, mostly on his own as his parents weren't really the type for big family get-togethers.

He looked at Jamie's wide grin and answered with one of his own, ripping off the last of the paper, looking closely at the present Jamie had gifted him.

A book of Christmas Carols.

Sheet music for his piano.

"Daniel can play that chopsticks thing on his piano," Jamie announced, his ten-year-old self not seeing a problem with the sudden silence that filled the room.

Daniel looked stunned at the gift and just ducked his head, Don and Sue exchanged stricken glances, and Megan was too busy eating her chocolate to speak anyway.

"What a lovely thoughtful present, Jamie," Sue said.

Jamie beamed and then turned expectantly to Daniel, waiting for his new brother's reaction.

"Thank you, Jamie," Daniel said softly, and placed the music book down next to him as if it burned him.

"Don't ya like it?" Jamie said, frowning.

"I love it, Jamie, but I haven't played the piano for a very long time," Daniel said so softly that Sue strained to hear.

"Well, come on then. Let's go do it now." And grabbing Daniel by the hand, he pulled and pulled until Daniel had no alternative but to at least stand, and grabbing the sheet music, Jamie started guiding him to the sunroom.

"Jamie, Daniel may not want—" Sue said to her whirlwind of a son.

"S'ok," Daniel said over his shoulder. He kind of felt he owed this family at least one nice thing from him at Christmas, for all of their tolerance and understanding in the past few months, and if he was made to play the piano well that was at least something he could do right.

Daniel slid onto the seat, running itchy fingers over the polished wood. Every week he came out and religiously polished it with the wood polish he had found under the sink, and the wood gleamed and felt smooth to touch. He slipped up the cover, his hands resting, hovering gently over the keys. Jamie thumbed through the book.

"Look," he said suddenly, placing the open face up on Daniel's lap. "'Away in a Manger'," he prompted eagerly. "S'for beginners. Can you do that? Can you? 'Cause I know all the words an' I could sing."

"Yeah, I can play it," Daniel said softly, his head starting to ache, taking the book from his lap and placing it in the correct position. He briefly glanced at the sheet music, remembering back to last Christmas and his renditions of music by Handel and Chopin for his mom's friend, in his role as their very own piano prodigy. Sue and Don arrived in the room, followed by a grinning Mark and a chocolate-covered Megan, and lowering his head, he gathered every reserve of strength he ever had in his ten years of life and began to play.

Heat built in his hands as movements, as familiar to him as breathing, pulsed and shone and sparkled as the music in his head was pushed out into the room. Beautiful, soft, hard, quiet, loud, a joy to the family around him, his fingers stretching to reach keys, hands speckled with freckles in a blur of motion as he played carol after carol.

Now Jamie wasn't stupid. He was going to see that Daniel wasn't even looking at the sheet music. He was playing from his head, and even if he was looking at the sheet music, then surely five verses of "Once In Royal David's City" didn't fit onto one page of sheet music, especially on the sheet entitled "Away In A Manger".

The family sang along to his music, mostly out of key, with lots of laughing and giggling, and Daniel felt the ice in his spine start to melt.

It was nearly midnight when Sue called a halt to proceedings, encouraging Don to take a sleepy Megan into his arms and telling Mark and Jamie to turn in. Daniel didn't move. He couldn't; he was on emotional overload.

She slid onto the stool next to him, putting her arm around him and hugging him close.

"I miss them a lot," he said brokenly.

"I know you do, Daniel; I know you do."

And then she did what she needed to do, just held him as he cried.

Now

Daniel washed and dressed in record time. He needed to get out of the house, preferably without seeing Jamie at any point.

He somehow managed it, kissing his mom goodbye, swiping a slice of Megan's toast so it looked like he actually wanted to eat something, mumbled something about practice, and then, grabbing his school bag, he literally ran from the house.

It had all gone so badly wrong. None of this was supposed to happen.

When he had come to the Walkers, it was just to come to terms with himself, certainly not so he could find a boyfriend. Definitely not so he could end up virtually jumping their son, leading him astray, make him think he wanted to touch Daniel in the intimate way he had.

Jamie didn't want this. He was confused, going through that whole angsty teenage thing. He was just a horny teenager needing release, and Daniel couldn't handle that.

If just this touch was causing his heart to break, then God help him if Jamie wanted to push it any further.

Suddenly he stopped his panicked walking as the solution hit him, and he stood as still as stone a few hundred yards from the school gates.

He would go. He had the credits. He would move, leave now, find somewhere near the college where he could stay, get a job. He could find his identity away from temptation and not lead Jamie astray. That would make everyone happy.

"Daniel… hey, Daniel!"

Daniel turned, relieved to see it was only Steve, his guitar strung over his back as usual. They had been friends so long;

a love of music and not being cool had brought them together, and his friend's smile was what pushed him over the edge.

"Steve, can I talk to you?" Steve would know what to do, Steve would help.

"'Course, you okay?"

Together they moved to sit against their tree.

"I don't know where to start."

"How about from the beginning," Steve teased.

Steve was the only person whom Daniel had confided in, and then only very briefly. "I kind of came out to the rest of the family."

"Jeez, did it not go well?"

"No, they were cool. It just had an effect I couldn't have foreseen by any stretch of the imagination."

"Jamie," Steve said simply, causing Daniel to look up at Steve, startled

"What do you mean 'Jamie'?"

"I don't know what I mean really, just that I often catch Jamie staring at you, an' it sometimes doesn't look brotherly. Know what I mean?"

"Oh my God." *How did I miss that?*

"I kind of think you need to talk to Jamie before it goes any further," Steve urged, catching Daniel's gaze. Seeing something there that must have worried him, he said, "Dan, tell me, what have you done? What has he done?"

Daniel couldn't answer, burying his head in his hands, Steve's words washing over him.

Chapter Twelve

JAMIE LOOKED OVER WHEN HE GOT TO SCHOOL TO THE TREE, seeing Daniel and Steve talking, then watching as Daniel dropped his face into his hands.

He waved at Tyler, narrowly avoided Lucy, who was definitely lurking with intent. Doubling back to the tree Jamie looked nervously at Steve, who just smiled at him reassuringly before leaving the two boys to talk.

"Dan." Jamie tried to make his voice gentle but insistent, and Daniel lifted his head, his beautiful gray eyes glassy.

"Jamie." Daniel's voice was thick and heavy with emotion

"You left without me." Jamie tried for a smile, but he knew it came off as weak.

"I needed to go. I'm sorry, I couldn't face… I just couldn't…"

"I know, I understand, honestly I do."

"Jamie, I'm really confused."

"Does it help if I say I'm not at all confused?"

"No, that just scares me, Jamie; it scares me a lot. That has always been you, confident, go-getting, knowing your own mind. That isn't me; I can't match that."

"I'm scared too, you know."

"Of what? Of Mom and Dad finding out?"

"No, well, yeah, I suppose that will be a difficult bridge to cross, but not one we couldn't manage together. No, the thing that scares me is that you are deciding in your freaky Daniel head this is going nowhere."

"My freaky Daniel head?" Daniel snorted.

"Yeah, it's a scary place, dude, and I bet it has already decided to leave home."

"Uh-huh, had that thought."

"What would that do?"

"Save you… from me… from these feelings…"

"Save me?"

"Yeah, you're confused, and I've probably done something or said something, and now you don't know what you're doing or anything, and it's all my fault." The whole sentence came out in one great rush of air.

"Jeez, Dan, what the fuck… Give me some credit here for knowing my own mind."

"Do you though, Jamie?"

"Yes, Dan, I do know my own mind. We need to talk. Can we at least talk, after school?"

"Yeah, we'll talk, Jamie, we'll talk."

"You know I love you, Dan."

"I love you too, Jamie… I do… you're my brother."

"We'll work this out, yeah?" Jamie said gruffly.

Daniel wished he felt as convinced as Jamie sounded they would work it out.

"I have drama practice after school, but I'll be home as soon as I can, and we'll talk, yeah?" Jamie said one last time before smiling softly at Daniel's frown and walking back to his friends. Daniel promised himself he wouldn't look at

Jamie as he left but did so anyway, a familiar heat pooling in his stomach.

———

LUCY WORKED her way to the tree area just as Jamie left and cursed her bad luck in not pinning the guy down yet for the prom. There might be three months to go, but she was going to the prom on the arm of the best-looking jock in school if it killed her. She couldn't look too desperate though. She needed to be careful.

Exasperated, she stood out of the morning sun in the shade of the tree, biding her time until second period English, wondering what Jamie had been talking about to geek boy. She had never seen such a serious expression on Jamie's face as she had just seen, and it amused her somewhat when she thought maybe pretty geeky Daniel was having girl trouble. She pitied the girl who linked up with Mr. Odd. Girl problems were certainly one thing his brother would never have once Lucy was in Jamie's life fixing it and keeping him in check.

She could almost taste prom queen, taste it so bad that it sent tingles up and down her spine.

———

STEVE MUST HAVE CAUGHT a peculiar expression on Daniel's face because he quickly slid back down next to Daniel when Jamie had moved off.

"You okay?" he asked cautiously, clearly not sure what had gone down.

"I'm cool..." Daniel started. Even he could hear the element of doubt in his voice.

"Is Jamie cool? Or is he being a dick about all of this?

"Yeah, he says we need to talk." Daniel screwed his face up, scrubbing his eyes with fisted hands.

"He's probably right, Danny." Steve had a smile in his voice; talking was always a good thing in his book.

Daniel raised his gaze to focus on his friend, raw, naked fear tumbling inside him. "Jeez, Steve, how can this all have happened so quickly? I mean I've struggled for years with the whole 'I'm gay' thing. But Jamie…"

"But Jamie what?"

"Jamie, Mr. Straight Basketball Star, suddenly decides he is gay as well and wants me?" He heard so much doubt, yet so much wonder in his voice. His head told him it wasn't true, but his heart desperately wanted to believe it could be.

They sat in companionable silence.

LUCY STUMBLED INTO THE GIRLS' restroom, the look of fury on her perfectly made up face enough to send three juniors chatting at the mirrors scurrying for their lives. Raw anger swelled inside her.

Her.

The injured party. How could he? How could Jamie do this to her? String her along? Play her for a fool?

How could he promise delights with views of his body and hide wicked lies in his heart?

She should have realized. She felt sick, horrified, let down, and so furiously angry she could taste blood in her mouth, copper and sickening. She pressed her hands to the sink, staring into the mirror, her eyes blinking back furious tears, and her brain working. There was no fucking way he was getting away with this, no way he was going to treat her like shit and not get some of it pushed back his way.

She would find a way. She needed to calm the hell down, pull herself together and… and… find Greg…

Chapter Thirteen

Then

DANIEL'S FIRST EVER MATH CLASS AT HIS NEW SCHOOL WAS A farce.

English, well, he aced that.

History, easy, his old school was terms ahead of what they were learning now at his new school.

Music, hmmm, didn't even need to try.

But math?

Math he hated; he always had. There was no art in it, no beauty in words or expression, no need to understand why or to innovate. It was all set down. Two plus two always equaled four, and it was excruciatingly boring.

But what killed it most for him?

They sat him next to a post-lunch Jamie at his hyperactive best.

Jamie, the math genius. The one child in the class who could actually see poetry in numbers, symmetry in solutions, and actually freaking enjoyed math. Add to that Jamie didn't need to try. Just like Daniel didn't need to try with music, or art, or literature.

"I'mma going to be a math teacher one day," Jamie suddenly confided in the exceptionally bored Daniel.

"Yeah?" he said, hoping that would cut the conversation dead.

"Yeah, 'cause math is easy." To Jamie's young brain, that was all he needed.

"Okay."

"Whatya going to do when you grow up?"

"I don't know."

"Oh."

And yet another famous Daniel conversation stopped, just like all the other times anyone wanted to talk to him.

He had loads to say. Inside, he actually had loads he wanted to say.

That he wanted to use his music and he wanted to be happy and he wanted to find out why he couldn't do math, and most of all, he wanted to find out why his mom thought it was okay to leave him alone.

Jamie just looked at him, his mouth slightly open, as if he wanted to say something, but then hesitating, looking at Daniel closely. Daniel just wanted to cry. Jamie didn't like Daniel crying, and it appeared to be his life's work to keep Daniel happy.

"Wanna play one-on-one at lunch?" he blurted out.

Daniel blinked at the sudden change in conversation.

"I can't, I've never…" Daniel gulped and visibly swallowed. How to admit that he had preferred piano to basketball?

"S'ok, I can show ya."

And so he did. They shot balls at the lowered hoop in the playground, Jamie patiently showing Daniel some moves,

Daniel fluffing them, Jamie encouraging, Daniel achieving, Jamie sharing the successes.

Just like life really

Now

Jamie shared fourth period AP math with Daniel. It was the only lesson they had timetabled together. Jamie was in the advanced group because of his innate natural ability with numbers, Daniel was in the same group only through focused hard work, determined for math not to be the only class he didn't excel in.

They didn't sit together. All through high school, they sat with their own group of friends. Daniel imagined it was a bit like twins who craved separate identities. He quickly accepted that he preferred the friends who wanted to work in lessons as opposed to Jamie's group who skated by on physical prowess or lucky skill in the subject. There was only one friend of Jamie's that Daniel liked, and that was Tyler, a guy who really seemed genuine. It was him that Daniel partnered with in AP math, while Jamie partnered with a short skinny brunette famous for her cheerleading abilities but whose name escaped Daniel.

Daniel had his head bent low over his exercise books, refusing to watch the door, not admitting he was waiting for Jamie to arrive but sensing the very second that Jamie walked in. He couldn't help it; he raised his head, waiting until Tyler slumped next to him before catching Jamie's eyes.

Jamie smiled.

Just the normal Jamie—Daniel exchange of smiles, nothing too obvious, nothing that spoke of hot and heavy and coming on each other and sighed gasps and exchanged kisses and breathing that pulled passion from their very centers.

Still Daniel blushed, and Jamie smirked, brushing past him to get to his seat, leaning into that cheerleader bimbo and saying something low that made her giggle.

Bastard.

LUCY FOUND Greg where he always was, under the bleachers with his football buddies, smoking something they shouldn't. Greg had been after her since eighth grade, but she had stupidly placed all her eggs firmly in the Jamie basket. She could still wind Greg around her little finger though; she just needed to play the right card.

She hid for a moment, remembering that time her mom wouldn't let her have those new red shoes on sale, forcing angry pathetic tears to her eyes, pinching her cheeks, biting her lips. Ready.

"Greg," she whimpered brokenly, stumbling towards him, his eyes going to her and widening in shock.

"Lucy, what the fuck? What's happened?"

"It's Jamie Walker… He, Greg, I don't know what to do, didn't know who else to talk to."

"What has he done, has he hurt you?" Greg held her away from him, checking for marks and bruises.

"Not physically. Greg, can we… can… can we talk?" and then she collapsed in sobs against his chest.

So far so good.

"Come on, come round here." Greg pulled her to one side away from his interested friends, pulling her into the protection of his strong arms. "Talk to me, Lucy."

"Jamie asked me to do something… I didn't want to…"

Greg immediately jumped to conclusions, adding two and two and making five. "Did he pressure you into sex, Lucy? Did he push you?"

"No, no, he wouldn't Greg... He won't... He has led me along all this time, lied to me, used me, and now I find out... I find out... Greg..." She raised her pretty violet eyes to his, bright and swimming with tears, her lips trembling, her face flushed. "He's been lying to me. He's gay, Greg. Gay."

"HEY, MRS. MONROE."

"Hey yourself, Jamie. Can you do me a huge favor and help move some of the scenery out? They need to get to the pipes at the back for the heating."

"Where to?"

"Just to the storage area. We can move it all back after practice. The guys said they won't be long."

Jamie quickly cleared the scenery, even volunteering to move it back after rehearsal. Mrs. Monroe called him a suck-up, but Jamie just grinned, knowing he would do anything for the drama teacher he adored.

It was difficult to concentrate on the rehearsal. He knew his lines, knew the direction, but his head was elsewhere. If it wasn't fighting memories of how Daniel felt coming apart in his arms, remembering the moans and the taste of him, it was thinking about the up-and-coming conversation he knew they needed to have.

Daniel had two colleges he was focusing on, but selfishly Jamie wanted Daniel to come with him to UCLA Arts, wanted him to get the place, accept the place, maybe share a room, share a life, work on this attraction... and this love he felt for Daniel. Start their lives together? God, he sounded

like some kind of chick who wanted to settle in the suburbs…
When had he turned thirty?

He knew it was going to be rough on his mom and dad,
but they loved Daniel and Jamie as separate sons, so why not
as a couple? It could work; it had to work. It just needed to be
talked through, and he had to make Daniel see they could
have a relationship, that Jamie wanted a relationship, that he
needed Daniel like he needed air.

"Jamie, where is your head at?" Mrs. Monroe laughed
tiredly. "Guys, I think we can leave it for tonight as Mr.
Walker is obviously not fully in the room." The group
sniggered, and Jamie blushed. "I have a staff meeting to go
to, guys. Let's meet up Tuesday and start again from scene
five, okay?"

A chorus of okays then everyone left, leaving Jamie to
move the scenery back on his own, a smile on his face and
happy thoughts in his head.

He shuffled around the pipes laid on the floor, his
movements clumsy and uncoordinated, humming under his
breath.

He didn't see his attacker, didn't hear his attacker, just
knew the pain of something hard and heavy across his head,
sending him to his knees, his eyes closing in reflex, his arms
going up about his head. The second hit was harder, a hand, a
boot, he couldn't tell, as it smashed into his ribs, his body
arching and rolling to one side.

"You fucking piece of shit," a voice growled in his ear.
There was another hit, this time a boot to his face, his neck, a
punch to his ribs. "You are one twisted… sick… boy
fucking… fag."

Another kick, this time to his throat, his chin. His head
was forced backward, and then he felt hands holding him
down, digging cruelly into his arms, cutting and scratching.

He felt his shirt being ripped to one side, something hot on his chest, a knife, cutting, pain so intense... His last conscious thought was of a need to escape, to run for help me.

Help me...
Help me.

Chapter Fourteen

THE AIR WAS HEAVY, AND JAMIE STRUGGLED TO BREATHE, desperately clawing at his throat as he sucked in vital oxygen. He wanted to call for help but couldn't form words. His hands were slick with blood, grasping for something to anchor against the agony in his head and throat. Noise was rushing in his head, white noise, his ears echoing. His eyes blurred with blood. He was dying and he knew it, but no one knew where he was. No one would look for him.

His body began to surrender as, bit by bit, his tenuous hold on consciousness slipped away. Damn if he was dying now. He just needed to move away from the shadows and into the light, just a few feet. His hands, wet with blood, couldn't seem to find purchase even as he hooked his foot around the corner of a door and, heaving, gave one last and final push to lay, finally, blessedly, unconscious on the cool hall floor.

Then

When Jamie acted in his first play in high school, the only person who knew he was doing it at home was Daniel. It had been Daniel he had bounced ideas off of, Daniel who explained and discussed and helped, and, more importantly, didn't laugh that the basketball jock was doing something so incredibly girly.

Jamie had been going through the whole "my parents expect me to get a ball scholarship when all I wanna do is act" thing. Daniel agreed he should try and supported, cajoled, and finally persuaded Jamie the rest of the family needed to know. Inevitably his family was fine with it, just wanting their son to be happy, even going so far as to book acting lessons for him.

They were all there at both showings of the play, enthusiastic and complimentary, but it was Daniel that Jamie looked for, Daniel who stood in the wings watching and mouthing the words alongside his brother.

It was just right.

Now

Daniel paced and then sat and then paced and then sat. Jamie should have been home at least an hour ago, and the fact he hadn't shown was surely a sign he had changed his mind. That he had realized what a bad thing he was doing with Daniel, how Daniel was leading him down a path he didn't want to go, and how he was now out there somewhere thinking up words to tell Daniel, to let him down gently. All Daniel wanted was the truth. He didn't think he could handle excuses or reasons now. He just wanted Jamie to be honest and tell him.

No, I don't. I don't want to see Jamie. I can't face him.

Yes, I can face him, Jamie is my brother.

No, he isn't just my brother. He is my whole reason for being, not just my brother.

Daniel stopped pacing, crouching down and reaching under his bed, pulling out the bags he used for camping and opened them.

Nothing too much, just the essentials: passport, cash, some clothes, a few books, his iPod, his photos, his memories, his family, his life.

I can't do this. I can't be here with Jamie, not after everything that has happened.

Yes, I can. I can live here with my family, not just Jamie's family, my family.

No, they'll just hate it. If they found out it was my fault, they would hate me.

Not thinking, he just threw what he could find into the bag, pausing only when he decided to pack the photos, images of happy times captured in glass frames.

"*Daniel!*" his mom called up the stairs.

He opened his door, moving to the top of the stairs. "Yeah, Mom?"

"Get Megan. That was the hospital. Jamie has been… there has been an accident… Dan, get Meg."

IT WAS a good hour before anyone came to talk to them.

"Mr. and Mrs. Walker?"

"Can you tell us what is happening?"

"Your son was brought in just after five. He was found at the school and has quite clearly been assaulted. He was stable when he was admitted, but there are injuries. He has three fractured ribs, his jaw is broken, and his throat has some quite serious tissue damage. What worries us most is the bruising to his head and face, which seems indicative of possible internal damage which won't make itself fully clear for a few hours. The police are, of course, involved, and we have taken photos of all the injuries. This is normal in any hate crime or crime with a possible homophobic motive."

"What do you mean?" Sue's voice tailed off.

"The detective in charge will want to talk to you. If you could all remain here, I will send him in." Then he continued to talk about medical details, but Daniel wasn't listening. A hate crime? Why would Jamie be a victim of an attack motivated by hate? No one hated Jamie. It was Daniel that deserved the hate; it was Daniel that was gay. He looked at Sue, knew what was in her head, could imagine it in her eyes. Why Jamie? It's the wrong son. Why not Daniel? He's not as important. He's gay, so why Jamie? And how the hell did anyone…

"Daniel, are you okay, sweetheart?" Sue asked, her voice tight and choked as she clutched Megan's hand.

Daniel couldn't even look her in the eyes, scared of what he would see. How could he answer that? What did they mean… hate crime… what photos? The energy to keep standing just evaporated, and he slumped into a chair, his head in his hands, ignoring Sue, knowing he had nothing to say in reply to her question.

"Daniel, they said he'll be okay, that—"

"Mr. and Mrs. Walker?" the officer said by way of introducing his presence in the room. Everyone looked up. "My name is Officer Dawson. I know you haven't been able to go in to see your son yet, but I am assured he is in good hands. I wanted to touch base with you to inform you we are treating this as a hate crime and have taken the appropriate action to begin investigations. This, of course, includes the crime scene, witnesses, and interviewing the family as a foundation to character and to compile a list of friends."

"What hate crime?" Mark suddenly snapped. "No one hates my brother."

"We often find in cases like this, where alleged homophobic attacks occur that—"

"Homophobic? I don't understand." This came from Sue. Daniel sank lower in his chair, the weight of his thoughts too much to bear.

"The scarring on his chest would point to the attack being motivated by sexual preference. Whoever did this to your son wanted to make the reason for the assault very clear."

"What scarring?" Don demanded, his voice strong and determined. He moved to gather a shaking Sue in his arms.

"The attackers, whoever assaulted your son, used a knife on your son's chest. They cut a word into the skin, three letters. F-A-G."

Sue let out a noise somewhere between a keening sob and *no*. Mark rose to his feet, echoing his mom; Don paled.

"It's me," Daniel blurted out. "I'm the fag; I'm the one that should be in that bed, not Jamie. He isn't gay." And then he couldn't stop. Blindly, he ran across the room and pulled the door to the bathroom open. He pushed the door behind him and, falling to his knees next to the toilet, lost whatever food was in his stomach, retching uncontrollably. His eyes burned with anguished tears, his unsteady hands gripping the cold porcelain, not believing what he had just heard. Who had done this to Jamie? Who knew? Only him and Steve. Who would… why… "Jamie… no."

He heard Mark's voice, Sue's voice. They were calling his name, trying the door. He couldn't do it; he couldn't face them. This was all his fault. They'd see that and then... then what? Then he'd get what he deserved... blame... He wasn't ready for that yet. He wanted to see Jamie... but Jamie's skin... his skin marked like that... why? Why would someone do that? Why scar him? How could he look in Jamie's eyes and not see blame and hate looking back at him?

"Daniel, they said we can see him. Do you want to go?" Sue called through the door, her voice fearful and filled with tears.

What do I say? I want to see him; I want to touch him, I want to tell him to his face that I'm sorry.

"I'm coming. I'm okay, give me a minute. I'll catch up with you."

"He's in recovery, Daniel. He'll want to see you if he is conscious."

"Okay."

If he's conscious, if...

Chapter Fifteen

DANIEL WATCHED UNNOTICED FROM THE DOOR. HE COULD SEE his mom hold her son's hand, blinking steadily as she catalogued every single scratch and mark and bruise. The cuts on his chest were bandaged, but every other injury was open to the world, for Sue to touch gently, tears on her face and her hands trembling. Don had taken Megan to the restaurant for coffees, and that left Mark, hunched on a chair next to his brother. They talked softly, their voices filled with disbelief, and Daniel stood and listened quietly at the door. Waiting for the conversation to turn to him.

"Maybe Daniel knows something?" Mark finally ventured, wringing his hands, his voice low and gravely.

"What? He was at home; he wasn't there?"

"Maybe, 'cause of… you know… how he is… Maybe he has been threatened, and Jamie stepped in. He would do that; he would protect Daniel."

"Yes, he would. Maybe that is what happened." Sue appeared thoughtful.

Daniel didn't want to break the illusion. He knew Jamie would have protected him, but he had to say what he knew.

"No one threatened me," Daniel said quietly, moving fully into the room. "No one knew. Only you and Steve. I hadn't said anything to anyone."

Sue jumped up, gathering Daniel into her arms. "Daniel, are you okay?"

"M'fine." He crossed to Jamie, his hands clenching and unclenching in a frustrated rhythm, wanting to shut his eyes, not wanting to see, but refusing to close them. He deserved to see this, to see how Jamie had been hurt.

It was so wrong. Jamie never stayed still this long. Even in sleep he moved, his long limbs taking up the bed, tangling sheets, but this stillness was awful.

He had to do something, see something. He focused on Jamie's face where bruises were starting to form around the cuts and abrasions, evil marks. They wanted to stop him. He sensed Mark moving. He heard Sue's intake of breath, but he held up one hand as he lifted at the corner of the taped bandage, pulling the tape back to reveal the deep cuts under it, orange with antiseptic, the word raw and jagged, letters not even formed properly, red against Jamie's pale, pink skin.

"Will it scar?" Daniel said softly.

"The doctor said it was unlikely it would scar as recognizable letters if it was looked after."

"But it will scar?" Daniel persisted, determined to hear the worst, determined to accept full blame for the worst.

"It may, yes." Sue moved to stand next to him, pulling his hand gently away from Jamie, pushing the bandage back in place, and holding Daniel's hand in hers. "Sit down, Daniel. He'll be awake soon, and he will want to see you here."

He won't; it's my fault.

IT TOOK Jamie another eight hours before he finally came

round. The specialist in charge of his care had been just on the edge of worried and was talking solutions like keeping Jamie in an artificial coma to give his head time to heal and offering possible scenarios if he didn't wake up. Added to that was the conversation he'd overheard between the two officers outside of Jamie's room, talking softly about manslaughter, murder, if Jamie didn't wake up.

Jamie *was* going to wake up; Daniel wouldn't leave his side until he did. He didn't repeat the conversation to Sue or to Don. He just spent time trying to understand why he wasn't thinking of them as Mom and Dad but as Sue and Don as they stood next to Jamie watching him slowly die.

It was nearly morning, dawn creeping into the room, when Jamie's first words split the silence. "Mom, Dad…"

There was a flurry of movement, the family banished from the room for a few moments before the doctor declared that Jamie was "holding his own".

"I don't remember. I didn't see anything," Jamie said to anyone that asked.

Then

"I've got something I need help with, Dan."

Daniel looked up from his biology homework, his eyes unfocused, blinking at the light falling from the hallway.

"Yeah?"

"Can you talk?"

"Uh-huh."

Jamie came into the room fully, pushing the door shut behind him.

"Is it one of those 'is it appropriate to wank in the shower' talks or a 'how far shall I go with Liz—Anna—Jane' talks?"

"No."

"What's up?" Daniel turned away from his homework.

"I've been thinking…" Jamie started, kind of nervously.

"Never a good thing." Daniel snorted.

"I'm sixteen, right?"

"Is that a trick question?" Daniel laughed, stretching back in his chair, that thin strip of skin between jeans and T-shirt flashing at Jamie. Jamie coughed, tearing his eyes away from his favorite view and floundered on into what he really wanted to discuss. His kind of weird attraction to his brother would just have to wait for another day.

"So yeah, sixteen, and a sure thing for basketball captain, yeah? Scouts have already talked to Dad from two colleges. I'm cool with a scholarship I think."

"Yeah, that's good," Nothing Daniel didn't already know. Jamie had been approached for his skill in basketball as Daniel was for his proficiency in music. Talent put both their names on people's lists.

"No, it's not good," Jamie said, sighing and slumping onto Daniel's bed.

"Okaaaaay… and a scholarship to a good college is a bad thing how?"

"What if it isn't what I wanna do?"

"Basketball is your life Jamie."

"No, not really. It's my skill; I'm tall."

"Freak."

"Shortass… anyway, I'm tall, and I'm good at basketball, but it isn't what I wanna do."

"So umm… what do you wanna do?"

"Act, become an actor, or maybe a drama teacher, I dunno."

"Jamie, is this 'cause of your crush on Mrs. Monroe? You do know she is married, yeah?"

"Daniel, no, I just… fuck, I don't know… but I need help."

"Medical help?"

"Ass, help to tell Mom and Dad."

"No."

"Seriously, dude, if you just cry or something…"

"I am not going to cry."

"Well, look supportive then?"

"I could do that I suppose."

"You *suppose*?"

"I'd need some kind of motivation."

"The undying respect of your brother?"

"I was thinking more along the lines of exclusive use on the PS."

"Shit, you're just going to practice level twenty-six so you can steal my high score."

"Deal or no deal."

"Shit."

Now

Jamie was aware of the people who had been in the room; he knew Mrs. Monroe had been in, her eyes suspiciously wet, her hands resting on his arm as if she needed physical contact to reassure herself that he was alive.

His mom and dad were a constant, and he knew Megan and Mark came in when they could, or more likely when they were allowed to. It was Daniel that was suspiciously absent. Daniel did visit. He visited with Mom, with Dad, with Mark and Meg, just never on his own, and the frustration of not being able to talk to Daniel alone was driving him insane. Today, the doctor had cleared him for going home the next day. He had been in hospital for four days, and not once in the time he had been conscious had Daniel mentioned anything about anything to do with the assault or their new feelings.

Tomorrow he would be going home, and it seemed as soon as Daniel heard this news, the tension in the room ramped even higher. It was just Daniel and Mom, and damn it, he needed to talk to Daniel. When they went to leave, Jamie asked Daniel to stay back a while. His mom frowned, her eyes flicking from Jamie's bruised face to Daniel's half-lidded eyes and back again.

"I'll meet you at home, Daniel," she said gently, dropping a small kiss on Jamie's head and promising to be there at ten a.m. on the dot for his release in the morning. She left, hesitating briefly outside the door. Evidently she was weighing up wanting to respect the privacy of her boys against wanting to unashamedly eavesdrop. She decided against listening and moved off down the stairs to the exit.

"JAMIE," Daniel said softly, "I'm sorry you got hurt" was all he could say, was all he wanted to say, as he began to back away to the door, almost reaching it, Jamie watching his every move. Jamie pulled back the covers, wincing at the pull in injured muscles, swinging, as much as he was able, his feet to the floor.

"What're you doin', Jamie?" Daniel said nervously, watching as Jamie grimaced in pain at every movement he was making.

"Followin' you. If you're leaving, I'm following 'til we

talk," Jamie managed to say, his voice gravely and low, his larynx still swollen and bruised.

"Jamie, please." Daniel could hear himself begging.

"M'not jokin', Dan." Jamie started to push himself up off the bed with his good hand, and it was all Daniel could do not to scream for a nurse.

He made a move toward Jamie, his hand out. "Jamie, no, I'll stay, okay? I'll stay and talk. Just, for God's sake, get back into bed." At his final word, he was at Jamie's side, helping him in, feeling the tension in Jamie's rigid form. When he had finally got his brother's gangly frame settled, he heaved a sigh of resignation. He had been trying to put this conversation off for days. It was going to be hard, but it needed to be done.

"Where is your head at?" Jamie asked suddenly. "Why won't you look at me, talk to me?"

Oh God. So Jamie leaps in with the really difficult question to start. "In a bad place, Jamie. You know as well as I do this was somehow attached to me, to us."

"No one knew about us," Jamie said softly

"Except Steve," Daniel blurted out.

Jamie smiled and shook his head. "Steve wouldn't say anything. He kind of knew anyway, about how I felt, and what he knew certainly wouldn't provoke him to assault me."

"I know but—"

"Dan, *who* doesn't matter. If you think about it, *why* doesn't matter either. All that matters is that we deal with this and move on."

"How? How do we move on when those… whoever hurt you… when they did it for that reason? How could I ever think that being honest would ever be the right thing to do?"

"Please don't, Daniel."

"Please don't what?"

"Don't leave me; don't go."

"I wasn't going to—"

"Dan, I know you. You think if you aren't here, that what? I wouldn't still want you? That I wouldn't want to spend time with you… together?"

"Yeah, maybe." Daniel's voice held a strange kind of aggression, not directed at anyone in particular, just at the world in general.

"Yeah, well, that is not going to happen. If you go, I'll find you, and we will sort this out."

"They won't want me to be here anymore, Jamie."

"Who? Our family? You think our family will cut you out?"

"They aren't—"

"Aren't what? Aren't your family? This is bullshit, Daniel."

"Will you let me talk, Jamie, please?" Daniel was close to crying. How the hell could he make Jamie understand this was his fault? That Jamie had nearly died because of him?

"Then talk, Dan, but for fuck's sake, try and make sense."

"Jamie, you… you nearly died…" He moved closer, his palm flat on Jamie's chest where he knew the scarring would be. "F-A-G. They carved that into you, so deep that some of it might scar. They left you nearly choking to death on your own blood. Tell me how you can rationalize that kind of hate, Jamie."

"You can't, Dan." He placed his own hand over Daniel's, pressing down against the bandage, knowing the hate that had been cut into him. "You will never be able to rationalize hate like that for religion, sex, gender. You can't rationalize what is inside someone that makes them want to hurt or want to kill." Daniel flinched at Jamie's words.

"I can't do it; I can't put you in this situation again."

"You didn't put me anywhere, Daniel. I chose where I wanted to be. Do you doubt that?" That was the problem; Jamie knew Daniel doubted Jamie had made the choice of his own free will.

"Maybe if I wasn't… maybe if I hadn't tried…" Daniel didn't know what to say.

"I was fourteen, Dan," Jamie blurted out suddenly, realizing this discussion was going nowhere.

"Fourteen?" Daniel wasn't following this new twist in the conversation.

Jamie blushed. "That is how old I was when I first realized I was maybe different. I felt strange. I saw how much I was part of you and you were part of me."

"You never said anything, Jamie."

"Neither did you, Dan. You never once mentioned you wanted me? I didn't know you were gay. Jesus, I didn't even know I was gay, not really. I just knew I wanted to get a lot closer to you than we were. I wanted to touch you, taste. Jeez, every fantasy I had in my head involved you."

"You were so young," Daniel mused softly, his hand warm under Jamie's.

"I was, I still am, we still are, Dan, and we have a whole life ahead of us."

"How long, Jamie? How long until someone guesses our secret and decides their hatred justifies violence again?"

"You can't tell, Daniel, what people are like; we can't tell. We don't know who did this to me. Who knew, who found out, who hated me this much? So what do we do? Get girls, go to college, live expected nine-to-fives, be unhappy?"

"Be safe," Daniel said stubbornly.

"Safe? Safe is dead, Dan; it is not living."

"I'm not brave enough, Jamie," Daniel said, trying to pull his hand away.

"I can help you, Daniel. We can be brave together."

"I… I…" Daniel stuttered, tears in his eyes. "I wasn't there when you got hurt; I wasn't there."

"And I am glad you weren't. I wouldn't wish this on you, but I'm glad it happened."

"Glad? Jeez, Jamie."

"Listen, if this hadn't happened, our secret would have gone with us to college. This way we can come clean, tell Mom and Dad—"

"No."

"Dan."

"No, I'm not… we can't… it's my fault…" This time he really was trying to tug his hand away, but Jamie refused to let it go, his nails digging into Daniel's skin. Daniel flinched but finally relaxed his pull.

"I want to look at it again," Jamie said, using Daniel's hand to pull the bandage back, Daniel trying to back away, shaking his head frantically.

"You can't. You can't see, Jamie, please don't."

"Get me to the mirror, Dan," Jamie insisted, his chest bare, his feet already swinging to the floor again, his body unsettled and swaying against Daniel. Daniel just held on tight, tears freely flowing down his face now. He didn't want Jamie to see what they had done, how his attacker had marked Jamie's chest with their hate. They reached the mirror, the taller boy stooped and clinging to Daniel tightly. They looked, at the red marks, at the cuts, the scabs, the stain of antiseptic.

Jamie considered the scar thoughtfully, his eyes heavy with much-needed sleep, his skin pale and wan.

"Daniel, promise me something."

"What, Jamie?" Jamie's tone of voice was scaring him.

"Promise me you don't give up on us, that we don't let them win?"

"I'll try, Jamie, I'll try."

"Daniel, something else."

"Yeah?"

"Can you help me back to bed? I think I'm going to pass out."

"Shit, Jamie, you dick." Somehow they managed to get Jamie back into bed, and it was with a certain amount of amusement that, when Mom came back in the room, the detective in tow, Jamie was half in and half out of bed. Daniel was swearing, and Jamie was muttering in pain.

"Boys," she said sharply.

Daniel turned a guilty face.

"I needed the bathroom, Mom." Jamie smirked, and between her and Daniel, they finally got Jamie back into bed.

"I wanted to be the first to say we have two people in custody for your assault," the detective said when Jamie was finally settled. "We have a—"

"It's Lucy and Greg." Sue was visibly vibrating with emotion.

Daniel paled, and Jamie looked disbelieving.

"Lucy?" Jamie stuttered. "Why would Lucy do this?"

"She hasn't said to date," the cop intoned, "but Greg has accepted his part in this and has been held over pending—"

"Pending what?" Jamie said suddenly. "What if I don't press charges?"

Sue gasped. "Why wouldn't you press charges?"

"In cases like this—" the cop started conversationally, but Jamie interrupted.

"Mom, no, I'm not looking for revenge here." Jamie looked at Daniel, his forehead creased in worry, his blue eyes bright with emotion.

"It's not about revenge, Jamie," Daniel said. "It's about accountability. Whatever the motivation, there needs to be some..." He watched Jamie's eyes fill with tears. All this time, he had never seen Jamie look so destroyed. "Jamie?" he said softly.

"Dan, you don't see, do you? If this... I don't know... people will know..."

"Jamie."

"Dan, they'll know about us, and you'll run, you'll go. I can see it now."

Silence descended.

Chapter Sixteen

"JAMIE…" SUE'S VOICE WAS NOTHING MORE THAN A whisper, her eyes wide and filled with shock.

The detective looked from one to another, his eyes taking in every nuance, every reaction. Deciding wisely that retreat was probably a good idea, he murmured something that no one really heard and backed out of the room, pulling the door to behind him.

"Mom." Daniel looked stricken, his eyes wide at the realization of what Jamie had just said, what he had revealed. He took a step away from Jamie, toward Sue, toward the door. Jamie caught his hand but was unable to keep hold as a white-hot pain shot up his arm. He inhaled sharply, and Daniel turned back to him, distress obvious in his eyes.

Sue just stood there. She hadn't moved yet, and Daniel slumped into the chair next to Jamie, his left hand searching and finding Jamie's. Jamie squeezed the hand hard, without taking his eyes off his mom.

"Jamie…" she began softly, tears shining in her hazel eyes, her lip trembling, her hands twisted in front of her. "How long?"

"Not long," Daniel said quickly, like his denial he had loved Jamie since he was much younger and newly arrived at the Walker's house would somehow help the situation.

"Jamie," his mom said sharply.

"Days, Mom. No more than days, but I have wanted it for a very long time."

"I don't understand. Daniel, you told us… was Jamie… you have to…" Sue looked pale, distracted, her hands moving to cover her mouth, the tears in her eyes falling down her cheeks.

Daniel stood and started to move toward her, knowing Jamie couldn't, but she held out a hand in a stopping gesture. He stopped.

"Sue," he whispered, not Mom; he couldn't say Mom. That single word—Sue—galvanized her to move, and she took a step closer to him, the boy she had taken in as her own son.

"I'm so sorry, I…" Daniel started helplessly, moved to his own tears by her tears, his heart breaking as he watched the stony anger banked in her eyes. He saw her hand move and felt it connect with his cheek. He heard Jamie shout, felt his own calm acceptance of her passion and her anger, expected it, wanted it, craved it…

"Don't call me Sue," she hissed, her voice choking with tears. "I am your mom, and Jamie… Jamie, is your brother."

"Mom, please."

Daniel heard Jamie's voice pleading behind him, but Daniel knew Sue was right. It was all wrong; everything was so wrong. He looked back at Jamie, saw him shaking his head in mute shock then looked back at Sue, his eyes carefully blank.

"M'sorry," he said, low enough so Jamie couldn't hear, and then he left. He pushed past Sue and just left.

"Daniel!" he heard Jamie call and imagined him struggling to get out of bed, imagined his mom stopping him, holding him back. He ran, weaving in and around people, his whole world collapsing around his ears. He heard his name, but he ran, blind, scared.

Then

Daniel had been with the Walkers three weeks and one day before he had his first panic attack. He had had them before, when his dad got sick, when his mom disappeared into her shell of fear, when his dad died, when his mom left him. But this one? This wasn't over anything big. It wasn't earth shattering or awful or the end of the world.

I can't do this, I can't do this, I can't do this.

He was pacing in front of his mirror, his school bag clutched tight in his hands, his breathing shallow, looking out from floppy, curly hair that covered his eyes, feeling his skin itching and his throat tightening.

"Daniel, we gotta go."

Daniel turned to his door. Jamie stood there, his arms crossed, impatience across his face, waiting for Daniel to get a move on.

Jamie... He tried to say it, tried to push it out past his throat... Jamie, I can't breathe. He knew Jamie was talking to him, could see him flailing his arms like a windmill but couldn't hear it all because of the blood rushing sound deafening in his ears. His legs buckled, his school bag still tight in his hands.

"Mom! Daniel is dying... Mom. Mom!"

The dizziness made him shut his eyes. If only he could

kickstart his breathing, but it wasn't working. His school nurse knew what to do.

"Mom. He won't open his eyes."

"Daniel, sweetheart… Jamie, get his bag… Daniel, I need you to calm down."

"Mom, stop him dying."

"He's not dying. Daniel, Daniel, breathe in and out, come on, sweetie, you can do this. Come on, Dan, breathe with me."

All the time Daniel could feel her, not holding him, not crowding him, just holding his arm, rubbing circles into his prickly skin as the sickness started to build in his stomach. His eyes filled with tears. He needed to be sick, he was going to be sick… He was sick, he was mortified, sobbing…

"Jamie, get your dad."

"Ewwww, Mom, there's sick everywhere."

"Jamie, get your dad… Daniel, keep breathing."

"I was sick, I'm sorry, I'm sorry…" Daniel was past mortified now.

"Don't, Daniel, don't worry."

"I'm really sorry. I won't do it again."

"Don, thank God, can you deal with the sick? Daniel, let's get you into the shower. Jamie, go to school."

"Mo-yom… Daniel needs to come too." Jamie was whining.

"Daniel will be at home with me today. I'll phone the school."

"But. He'll miss show and tell. It's family day. Emma is bringing in her sister Emily, and she's only two days old, and she's really tiny, and I wanted Daniel to see my photos—"

"Jamie, enough, go to school."

Daniel showered and changed with Sue's help. She then wrapped Daniel under the Star Wars quilt in Jamie's room.

"My poor, poor baby," she crooned into Daniel's hair as he cuddled in close to her. He must have felt like he didn't have a family left to show and tell. "It's okay. It's going to be okay…"

Now

Mark was there, catching him, stopping him. "Daniel, stop, Daniel, dude, what's wrong. Oh my God, is it Jamie?"

Wait? What had Mark said? Jamie? Daniel pulled himself out of his despair, his hurt, his anger, his fear, and looked, just looked at Mark, and saw fear in his eyes.

"No, God no, m'sorry… left him upstairs… Sue… with Mom."

Mark visibly relaxed. "Then what the hell is wrong?"

"I can't Mark, I can't…," Daniel felt his chest restrict, the air thick and heavy around him, his hands up at his throat, desperately trying to gasp in air.

"Jesus, Dan, what the fuck?"

Daniel hadn't had a panic attack in years. It was Jamie who sat with Daniel, who calmed him down, normally.

"I can't… can't breathe."

Mark pulled him into a semi-hug from the side, pulling him to sit down on the floor in the corridor, their backs to the walls, gently rubbing small circles on his knee and firmly and clearly directing his breathing. "Slow, Danny, in, out, in, out, steady, in…"

Daniel focused on the words and tried to blank his thoughts, tried to focus, but all he could see was the shock in Sue's eyes, shock that he knew would be in Mark's eyes at any moment.

"Let me, Mark... Daniel, it's Mom, sweetheart... I'm sorry... I'm so sorry."

He heard the words then felt softer hands and gentle touches.

"Mom," Daniel said, in a desperate breath, burying his head in Sue's neck.

"Always, sweetheart, always your mom. I'm so sorry. I never should have done that. I didn't mean it; I didn't mean to hurt you. Now breathe, sweetheart, breathe."

Mark moved up off the floor and into a crouch. "What the hell is going on?"

"Go sit with your brother, Mark. Be sure to tell him we are okay. Quickly now."

"Mom, tell me. What's happened?"

"We'll be fine, Mark; we'll be fine."

Chapter Seventeen

MARK FLEW INTO HIS ROOM IN A FLURRY OF MOTION AND moved to Jamie's side.

"Jamie, what the fuck is going on?" Jamie turned his head away from his brother. He couldn't stop the tears and cursed the fact he couldn't move. "I saw Dan—"

"Is he okay?" was Jamie's quick response, his head sharply turning back to face his older brother.

"He's okay now. He had a panic attack. Mom is with him."

"Mom?"

"Yeah, I had him regulating his breathing, and she kind of took over, sent me up here. She has him calming down now."

Jamie shut his eyes tight, desperately willing his cramping muscles to relax. Hearing his mom was with Daniel was a good thing.

"Were they talking?"

"Not much talking, bro. Daniel was barely coherent when I left him."

"Shit... Was Mom... Was Mom..." He searched for the

right words, but he really didn't know what to say. Mark swung the chair around at the side of the bed and straddled it.

"Jamie, you wanna tell me what's going on? Why Daniel has had his first panic attack in years? Why are you crying?"

"It's really difficult, Mark. I'm not sure I can—"

"Bull. Shit. Jamie. Tell me or I'll take away your pain meds."

"Mark, I think I'm gay." There, he'd said it fast, like ripping a bandage from skin, quick and pain free. Mark's mouth fell open, and he sat for a few seconds taking in what Jamie had said. A myriad of emotions passed over his face, confusion the main one.

"Gay?" he repeated.

"Gay."

"Gay like Daniel," he said, because of course he needed this defined in a way he could understand.

"Kind of gay *for* Daniel."

"Oh. So that is why Daniel is so upset? Does he think Mom is saying it's Daniel's fault or something? She wouldn't do that."

"I kind of blurted it out, and it hit Mom at the same time she found out who had assaulted me, and I think it was overload. He called her Sue. Not Mom. She was in shock, and she slapped him."

"Shit, no wonder Dan panicked. He must feel like she was…" Mark twisted his fingers into his hair.

"Saying that he had turned me gay?" Jamie said bluntly.

Mark winced. "I guess."

Silence fell between the two brothers, each deep in thought. Jamie could see the way Mark's mind was working, knew he was trying to process the Walker kids had a fifty percent hit rate on being gay and wondering how it had all crept up on him. Mark had always been a good brother, an ass at times, but always there when Jamie or Daniel needed him. Jamie wondered if he had lost that now.

"How do you feel about it all?" Jamie finally plucked up the courage to ask as he slipped down in his bed tiredly, wishing with everything that Daniel would come back.

"I'm cool, little brother. I kind of thought what you and Daniel had was very close, never real brothers, just the closest friends I had ever seen. It's not going to be easy. This —" Mark waved a hand at Jamie's bed. "—is just the start of the crap that is going to be piled your way."

"I know, Mark, we haven't decided on this on a whim. We haven't really started anything, in fact; this is all new. I want to talk, and Daniel is avoiding it."

"Sensible guy," Mark said with a smirk. "Your talks never make much sense."

"Ass."

"Jerk."

"So me and Dan…"

"Whatever, little brother. I'll freak out, of course I will, 'specially when it comes to the horizontal dancing—"

"Mark…" Jamie started to blush, exhaustion sweeping over him as his latest pain meds started to take effect.

"But, y'know, you'll be at college soon. Maybe it'll be a better environment for the two of you than senior high."

"Uh-huh." Jamie was fighting sleep, but as much as he tried to stop it, it was pulling him under.

"Jamie, you asleep?"

"Uh-huh."

DANIEL'S BREATHING finally slowed long enough for him to gather his thoughts. He pulled back away from his mom, wincing as he looked up at her. She touched him gently on the face where she'd hit him.

"Can you forgive me?" she asked softly.

"Mom."

"Can you?" she insisted gently. He nodded, fresh tears in his eyes.

"It's me that's sorry, Mom," Daniel said brokenly, his voice heavy with tears.

"You haven't done anything, Dan. I was in a strange place there. I heard what you said, but I didn't listen."

"Mom, it's okay."

"I don't know how that's happened to me. I lost control, and I hope one day you can forgive me for losing my way there."

"There isn't anything to forgive," Daniel whispered, burying his head in his mom's neck.

"It'll be okay, Daniel. We'll get your dad here, and we'll talk, and everything will be okay. You'll see." She murmured reassurances into his hair, her hands steady on his back, letting him sit a while.

"Can we go back to Jamie?" Daniel finally said. "Am I still allowed to see Jamie?"

"Of course you are, sweetheart. You go up, and I'll be along in five minutes. I need to phone your dad." They stood, each looking into uncertain eyes. "Go on, Daniel. Tell him it will all be okay, and that we can work it out."

Daniel nodded and returned to the stairwell, casting one look back at his mom, standing resolute in the sea of new arrivals and people leaving to go home. She kind of looked lost for a moment, and then he saw the steel in her as she straightened her spine and walked out of the front door, her cell phone in her hand.

He climbed the three flights of stairs slowly, knowing

Mark was in the room, knowing Jamie would have had to say something. Carefully, he pushed open the door, taking in the room, seeing Jamie asleep and Mark standing in front of the window looking out at the street below. Mark half turned and smiled as the door shut behind Daniel.

"You okay now?" Mark asked gently. When Daniel suffered a panic attack, it often left him unsteady for hours.

"M'fine, Did Jamie… was Jamie…" *Jeez, how difficult is it to just come out and say it.*

"Jamie told me he is gay, that he is gay for you, then you called Mom Sue and not Mom, and that she slapped you."

"Oh."

"And before you say anything… Shit, Daniel, could you two maybe have chosen an easier path in this world?"

"I can't. I didn't." God, he wasn't making any sense. What could he say? That they had done little more than kiss? That Jamie wanted to talk and Daniel wanted to hide? That they weren't actually a couple, not really?

"Dan, you don't have to say anything. Jamie is sleeping, and I'm watching. Lie down on the other bed and get some rest, you look gray." Daniel smiled a half smile and crossed to the other bed, afraid to look too closely at Jamie.

———

WHEN JAMIE WOKE UP, it was to that peculiar hospital darkness, artificial low-level lighting casting eerie shadows around his room. He blinked, aware of someone breathing in the room with him.

"Mom?" he asked softly

"No, Jamie, it's me."

"Dan, what you doing here still?"

"Your mom went home, Mark too. Dad came and

collected them. I won't leave, and you were too out of it for the big family discussion."

"What did I miss?" Jamie's voice sounded gruff still.

"We'll all talk tomorrow. At least everyone is talking about it, Jamie." He moved to Jamie's side, holding his hand, helping him to sip water, stroking his hair, dropping a soft kiss on his dry lips.

"Are we going to work this out?" Jamie asked fearfully, his chest tight with worry.

"We're going to try, Jamie. I promise we're going to try."

"And you won't run?"

"I won't run."

Chapter Eighteen

THE SILENCE IN THE CAR WAS OPPRESSIVE.

Jamie was sitting in the back, and his dad was driving. He hadn't said much to Jamie. He'd hugged him, told him it was going to be okay, helped him into the car and then spent the time in the car humming along to big band music on some crummy station that would normally have Jamie trying to switch it. Jamie knew what was inside his dad. Probably disappointment and shock that his macho basketball captain son was suddenly confessing undying love for his brother. He imagined his dad, driving and at the same time trying to figure out if he had done anything wrong and even, as the father figure, if he was responsible for it all. That would just be so typical of him, to try and take the blame even when there was nothing like that to apportion.

Jamie knew what he would find at home. Family conference. Mark would be there, smirking, as it was Jamie and Daniel at the root of this discussion, and Mark knew it. Megan would be there. She was old enough to participate, although their last conference, over the mystery of the broken television, had been lighthearted and even that had made her cry. His mom would have made cookies; she always did. She said discussion was always easier on full stomachs, and the cookies always came with coffee or chocolate. The rule was simple. Each person had their say, uninterrupted, and when everyone had said their bit, they discussed the situation.

Jamie was in pain. Distracted by both the pain and the conflicting emotions inside of him, he couldn't find the words to say what he'd meant at the hospital, and he just felt frustrated and angry at himself. It was just... dealing with guys, with emotions, with his father, his brother...it just wasn't easy. There was an uncomfortable feeling buried deep inside of him, soaking in the discomfort from his dad, the anguish from his mom, the sad acceptance from Daniel...

How could he even begin to catalog the reactions and make sense of them?

And really... was he actually gay? Or was he literally just in love with Daniel, and that would be it for the rest of his life? He hadn't meant to create this mess. It wasn't like he'd chosen to upset everyone; it wasn't like he ever meant Daniel to know how he felt. He never wanted to show anyone the result of this strange insidious snake of feeling and emotion that curled in his belly and made him want.

When the car stopped outside the house, he saw they all stood at the door, even Daniel, waiting for Jamie to get home. Daniel wouldn't meet his eyes. He mumbled something into a halfhearted hug, before pulling away and walking into the kitchen, taking his normal seat. Jamie followed, sitting opposite him. Mark jostled and pushed Megan to get to their seats, finally swinging her up and over him, tickling her, forcing giggles past her smiling lips. Lastly, Dad sat down, and Mom passed drinks and placed a plate of cookies in the middle.

"Are you okay to be doing this, Jamie?" she asked softly.

All eyes moved to Jamie, each person uncomfortably aware that Jamie was clearly in pain and this was going to be hard.

"I'm fine. I need to get this all out in the open. We each need to have our say like we usually do," he said clearly. "If it is okay with all of you, I want to go first." No one argued. Daniel opened his mouth as if to say something and then subsided into silence, his eyes staring down at the table, his fingers twisted together.

"I don't know what to say really, where to start…" He hesitated, wringing his hands in front of him. Did he love Daniel? Was it actually love or just a fascination that would die? Was it forever? He had to be sure before he made it final. He was sure he knew what he wanted, but weighing it against peace, against normal, how could he push it so far? "I know what I feel… I know what I want. I want to be with Daniel," he started simply then dropped his gaze, his heart pounding, his stomach churning. Daniel couldn't even look him in the eyes. "I know it isn't going to be easy. I know I am setting myself up for all kinds of heartache, but…" He stopped, concentrating on the dark color of the coffee, his hands burning where they cupped the mug. He couldn't speak. He could feel he was shaking, the pain meds from earlier starting to tail off.

"Jamie, do you want to do this another time? You look so tired and gray," his mom said softly. Jamie simply looked at her, shaking his head almost imperceptibly.

He continued, "I hope that whatever I choose… whatever Daniel and I choose… that we will always be able come back here and feel safe. I don't want to scare you, any of you, and Daniel… with any of this… with how I feel…" He stopped again, his eyes bright with tears, his voice choked and stuttering. "I just know I don't want Daniel to leave, to feel he has to leave without me… Please don't leave, Daniel." Jamie fell quiet, tears running down his cheeks, looking directly at Daniel willing him to look, wanting to see his gray eyes. He wouldn't look up. *Please look at me.*

"I have something to say," Mom started softly, squeezing her husband's hand for reassurance. "I want to apologize to Daniel for the awful way I reacted at the hospital. He knows I am sorry. I have no real excuse other than the shock of finding everything out in the space of a few seconds. "

"It's fine," Daniel said quietly.

"I am terrified that a relationship between the two of you will open you to a lot of pain. Pain that your dad and I won't be there to help with, hurt and unkindness that we can't stop. It is our job as parents to protect all of our children, and if we aren't there…" Her words stopped, tears thick in her voice. Don turned to her, returning the reassuring squeeze. "If we aren't there, we can't stop the hurt."

Dad looked at her, his gaze filled with sadness and anger.

"In my heart, Jamie, Daniel, all I want is for you to be happy, both of you," he started softly. "I can't deny it is a complete shock that you seem to have suddenly decided you are gay, Jamie, especially after Daniel's announcement. I wish I could just accept this at face value, but I can't…" He paused. "I need time. We all need time I think." He evidently had nothing else that he could put into words.

"Dad?" Jamie wasn't sure what he was asking. His dad's expression was so sad.

"It breaks my heart that my sons' lives are going to be hard and that you're choosing a path that was so very different from what is expected. That's all." No one said anything in response. It was Mark's turn to talk, and he appeared to be thinking hard.

"I guess I haven't got much to say really," Mark finally said into the silence. "I've already spoken to Jamie, and Dan knows how I feel. It's going to be hard, I know that, but they have my support if that is what they want." He shrugged. He had nothing else to say, and in his mind, he had clearly covered it all.

So the only person left. Daniel.

"Daniel?" Jamie said softly. "Say something."

Daniel lifted his face finally, looking directly at Jamie, gray eyes clear and bright with unshed tears and a wealth of emotion. He blinked steadily, a small smile on his lips, his breath even and soft. "I don't have much to say... I mean, when it was just me... I could kind of handle that, but you as well... the two of us? That scares the life out of me." He paused. "You know that, as our brother, Mark will get shouted at, singled out for abuse, and Mom, you and Dad will have hateful things said to you, and Meg... Megan, she'll have stuff she'll have to handle too."

Megan shrugged and smiled, and Jamie wondered how much his little sister understood.

"Jamie, if we do anything, if it goes... I don't know... Can we hold off until after graduation, when we are at college where we can try and keep ourselves private and separate? If you promise to do that, then I promise not to run."

Jamie wanted to say no, but he knew things would be tense and uncomfortable there for a while, that the family dynamic would only be salvageable by love.

After everything that had happened, Jamie didn't hesitate. "Okay," he said softly, firmly, his heart pounding in his chest. "We keep it private, just ourselves, and you don't run. I can do that, Dan, I can do that."

Everyone at the table fell silent as they became lost in their own thoughts.

"Is it my turn?" Megan piped up. They all turned expectantly toward Megan. She was, after all, entitled to her say. Sue had tried to explain as much as she could, but she was ten; it was difficult.

"Go on, Megs," Jamie encouraged.

"So, Daniel is gay, which means he likes kissing boys, and Jamie is gay 'cause he likes that too, and they like kissing each other, which is kind of way cool. I just I wanna ask something though… I wanna know when Mark is going to be gay too."

IT WAS three weeks before Jamie could return to school. Lucy and Greg were conspicuous by their absence; no one said anything to Jamie about why he had been attacked. He knew there was speculation, but he was not going to fan the flames any more than had already happened.

The three weeks at home had been torture.

He and Daniel had talked and talked and then talked some more. There was a bit of kissing, but the actual physical side of their growing relationship was on hold out of respect for the rest of the family, Jamie's injuries, and their own wish to take it slow.

Problem was a week away from Daniel's eighteenth birthday he received two acceptance letters. One from UCLA Arts. One from Juilliard.

"It's no competition," Jamie said softly. He leaned back against the shady tree in the yard. Keeping his eyes carefully blank of emotion, he schooled his features to relax into an attitude of calm acceptance. New York. California. Worlds apart. "We can visit on holidays, and Skype."

"I've been thinking a lot about Juillard," Daniel said, his head tipped back, resting back onto Jamie's shoulder, the two letters in his hands. "Did you know it's fifty thousand dollars for the first year at Juillard?"

"You have the money, don't you?"

"Enough for maybe three years. But I didn't qualify for a scholarship, not a full one, and it's four years. It isn't the money though."

"Then what is it?"

"I'm not ready for it, Jamie. I love my music, I love playing the piano, but I'm not ready for it to define my life any more than basketball defines yours. I don't have the heart for it, the passion for it, I think maybe…" Jamie curled a hand on his arm, applying light pressure reassuringly. "I think maybe, I was so focused on the playing, on pleasing my mom." He shrugged, turning his face in to Jamie's neck, feeling the warmth and smelling the scents of soap and clean laundry.

"Don't do this just to please me then," Jamie said softly, his voice breathless with some unnamed emotion.

"I'm not, Jamie, not really. When my mom left, when she killed herself, she took the passion I had for music and turned it on its head. There was still passion there, I still had it in my heart, but it wasn't love. It was hate and revenge and self-loathing. Years of counseling doesn't change the fact I have all that inside me."

"So what will you do? What choices will you have?"

"I'm going to accept UCLA Arts. It's early to choose my path in life, but I have really thought about this, and I want to… hell, you're going to laugh."

Jamie pulled him impossibly closer. "No, trust me, I won't. I mean, look at me. Basketball playing drama teacher, yeah, right."

"Don't put yourself down, Jamie. You'll be an awesome teacher one day, or an actor if that's what you wanna do. Me? I've been looking into music therapy, y'know helping kids like me who need it, with music."

Jamie could feel Daniel's blush, his skin heating. "God, Dan, that is brilliant."

"Well, I'm going to try. They have a therapy department attached to the college, and I've already spoken to some people." Daniel's voice was muffled against his neck, but Jamie still heard the underlying excitement.

"So, both of us at UCLA Arts. We could, y'know, maybe share a dorm room or an apartment."

"Yeah, I was kind of thinking the same thing."

"A fresh start, just us, the two of us."

"Yeah."

"Awesome."

Chapter Nineteen

DANIEL'S EIGHTEENTH BIRTHDAY FELL ON A FRIDAY A FEW short months after Jamie's. It was family and a few friends and a barbecue in the garden; it was music and laughing and celebration and announcements. It was lazy kissing in Daniel's room; it was nothing more than peace and contentment.

It was the Saturday that changed the whole pace of the Jamie—Daniel relationship.

With Sue and Don's wedding anniversary and Mark back to college, Jamie and Daniel were babysitting the irritable and, quite frankly, exhausted Megan, who fell asleep on Jamie's lap by nine. They put her to bed, leaving them alone, awake, inventive, and with enough teenage male testosterone floating about to fill a stadium.

After collecting drinks, locking the house, checking on Megan, checking the house again, they finally crept into Daniel's bed, climbing embarrassed and in pajamas under the covers, curling into each other, comfortable with years of brotherly hugs, but oh so aware of every inch of bare skin that touched in this new definitely non-brotherly way.

It was Jamie that made the first move, always Jamie, as he rolled half on top of Daniel, his dick already hard against Daniel's hip.

"We're not doin' this," Daniel protested softly, at the same time his hands unconsciously gripped hard at the material gathered at Jamie's hips.

"I won't tell anyone," Jamie whispered back "I've waited so long for this, just to touch you, to kiss you."

"Jamie, I think—"

"Stop thinking, just for five minutes, yeah?" He moved his face until they were inches apart, Daniel's gray eyes looking uncertain and almost scared. "Close your eyes, Dan." Immediately Daniel closed his eyes, his lips parting on a sigh as Jamie dropped small tasting kisses to his mouth, touching his tongue gently to Daniel's. Even that small taste was enough to elicit a groan from the older boy.

Kissing and touching and laughing, hands moving and searching, their relationship was comfortable and familiar. Jamie aligned his body, rolled farther on top of Daniel, so close, so hard against each other, needy.

Breathless kisses exchanged with soft murmurs led to hands that searched and moved, Daniel pushing Jamie slightly away and tracing patterns on his chest, concentrating on the nipples. Jamie arched away, a muffled groan in his throat, pushing his dick against Daniel.

"That is…" Jamie started breathlessly. He never finished the sentence as Daniel pushed the touch, harder, firmer, more directed. Jamie actually whined in his throat. His dick was impossibly hard, and he was so very close.

"Jamie," he begged, the words muffled in Jamie's mouth. "Please…" He wasn't even sure what he was asking for, what he needed, but he was so close. "Your hands, Jamie, please… damn… please."

Jamie heard him, stopped his movement then traced his hands across Daniel's chest. They traveled lower, and he wrapped his hand around both of them. Swallowing Daniel's muffled pleading and fighting his instinct to go fast, he began to move slowly. Daniel didn't last much longer than he did, and it was incredible to see Daniel's face taut, his neck thrown back at the peak of pleasure. It was an image erotic enough to send Jamie tumbling after Daniel, losing it across his hand. He slumped against Daniel, both breathing heavily, and then Daniel offered words to the darkened room…

"This is just the start. We can have more."

PROM WAS AN INTERESTING SITUATION. Daniel wasn't going. It meant nothing to him. If he could have his way, the prom would be cancelled. He wanted to shout from the school roof that Jamie had been hurt, that they all needed to take the blame. Why couldn't people accept different? But he didn't. He didn't say a word.

Jamie was going. On his own. Not with a girl. Not with Daniel. When Daniel pushed him, Jamie admitted it was because he wanted to show people he had nothing to hide, that his jock side needed to show everything was normal and that he didn't give a shit he had almost died.

Daniel argued. "Nothing is normal, Jamie. We don't belong here anymore."

Jamie insisted, saying he didn't expect Daniel to understand why he had to go. "I need to face the ghosts, Dan. I need to show people I'm not scared of what anyone thinks or does." It was a heated discussion with Daniel refusing to go and Jamie determined to go. Neither convinced the other.

Chapter Twenty

Daniel knocked on Jamie's door.

"Jamie, can I come in?" he asked softly. As he waited for the sound of Jamie's voice, the door swung open.

"You don't need to knock," Jamie said softly, his hands at his neck, trying to fix his tie. Daniel couldn't find his voice. Jamie in jeans and a T-shirt was hot, Jamie in sweats after a basketball game was hot, Jamie in a rented tux… hotter.

It had been a hard few months. Jamie had been left with some problems as he healed, in particular a fine scar that ran down the left side of his face and a fractured knee that had ruined his chances for a basketball scholarship. The scarring on his chest had healed a bit more, and the letters had lost their definition, for which Daniel was forever thankful despite Jamie's matter-of-fact statement it was a badge of honor. The kids at school had looked at Jamie differently, no longer as a jock, but as a vulnerable teen. Some said he was gay, and that is why he was beaten up. The full story had come out in the last week.

Lucy admitted she had told Greg lies, admitted she had encouraged Greg to think Jamie had been leading her on while lying behind her back. She had been held for psychiatric tests and had disappeared from the school on a permanent basis. Evidently her parents had taken a plea bargain, and she was being homeschooled on probation. Greg had been released to his family but hadn't been seen back at school since his arrest. His future was trashed, his college placement hanging in the balance, and his parents devastated. He had accepted his part in the attack, admitted he had been motivated by some kind of displaced macho revenge. He had even written a letter to Jamie explaining, apologizing… begging for some level of forgiveness.

Jamie received the letter the same day he heard from the hospital that his knee would never heal enough for him to play professional basketball. It hardened his heart.

School had been hard simply because "normal" had ended so suddenly. Daniel still sat with his friends, but Jamie had taken to sitting with them. In fact, the first day back at school, he stood thoughtfully between two tables, jocks and geeks. It took seconds to decide where he really wanted to be, and he settled in a chair next to Daniel, bumping his shoulder and exchanging nods with Steve. No one said a word when Tyler picked up his tray from his usual seat on the jock's table and came over to slide into the chair opposite Jamie.

"S'okay?" he said softly. No one said anything. Jamie looked at his friend, sensing the quiet around them that this defection from the jock table had caused.

"S'ok," he replied softly. He had Daniel, he had Daniel's friends, and he had Tyler. He didn't need basketball. It didn't define his life. He had enough here, and he felt calm and settled and protected.

Prom plans had continued. Lucy might have disappeared, but her shocked friends had shouldered the mantle of organization, and it was scheduled for the beginning of May.

Jamie stayed out of it. He wanted nothing to do with it and kept his head down.

He spent one rainy Saturday afternoon with his mom and dad looking at his options. His place at UCLA Arts had been partially funded with the basketball scholarship, but that wasn't a problem. He had money from his grandmother.

Daniel spent the entire discussion pacing outside the kitchen doorway. He had money; he had lots of money. Sure it was tied up with so many provisos on what it should be used for until he was twenty-one it made his head spin. Still, he had been left enough by his own parents' life insurance policies to keep him comfortable. He wanted to jump in and hand the whole lot over to the Walkers. They wouldn't let him. He couldn't understand their reasoning and vowed to himself he would find a way to give the money to them one day. Jamie wrote his acceptance letter to UCLA Arts and figured on a new start to life. Daniel wrote his regrets to Juilliard, wrote his acceptance to UCLA Arts, and they posted their letters on Sunday.

And now prom had arrived. Jamie stood in front of him in a suit, fiddling with his tie, and muttering something about torture as he turned back to the mirror. Daniel slumped down on the bed, watching his... boyfriend... get ready. He was gorgeous, sexy and all Daniel's. In his heart, he knew he was doing the right thing by not going he just hoped he didn't fuck it all up. He had other issues he needed to come to terms with, places to visit, people to see.

"I wish you were coming with me," Jamie said softly, meeting Daniel's eyes in the mirror.

"I know, Jamie, I know." Daniel smiled. "It's not my thing."

"I'll miss you tonight."

"No you won't, Jamie; you'll have Tyler." Daniel tried to lighten the situation, but Jamie was having none of it.

"I. Will. Miss. You. And I will be home as soon as I can."

"You look amazing, Jamie," Daniel said quickly. He crossed to stand next to Jamie, who in turn pulled him into a quick hug, laughing as Daniel immediately buried his face in Jamie's neck, kissing his skin. Jamie moved into a kiss, soft and searching, both almost instantly hard. Jamie reached to cup Daniel's face, angling his head to get a taste. Daniel just whimpered at the sensation of being held, his own hands curling in the front of Jamie's shirt.

Daniel locked his hands behind Jamie's back and hugged hard, hoping that Jamie would forgive him for what he was doing tonight.

"Jamie, Tyler is here." Their mom's voice echoed up the stairs.

"Coming, Mom."

"Tyler is picking you up?" Daniel asked curiously.

Jamie shrugged. "Well, Tyler and April are picking me up."

"Poor April." Daniel smirked.

Jamie thumped him on the arm, snagged his jacket, and left the room, taking the stairs carefully, his knee stiff and sore. Daniel followed him and then stopped at the top of the stairs. With a short wave, Jamie disappeared out the door. Daniel waited a good five minutes before going downstairs. He had to be sure Jamie had gone.

Sue was at the door, Don at her side, watching as Daniel came down the same stairs, duffle in one hand, laptop in the other. She looked sad, and Daniel could have sworn she was going to cry.

"Mom," he said gently, standing in front of her, his

shoulders back, his eyes free of tears. He didn't want anyone to think he doubted the wisdom of this journey.

"Daniel, you promise you will be careful," she said, pulling him into a hug. "Do you have your phone? And some money? Don, give him some money—"

"Mom, I have money, I have my phone. I'm only going to be a hundred and fifty miles away. I'll be back before you know it."

"Phone us and let us know when you get there."

"I will."

"We love you, Daniel."

"I love you too."

"Promise you'll phone."

"I promise."

He gave his dad a quick hug, picked up his bags, and walked out the door toward Mark's old Toyota. He looked back for a final wave before starting the engine and pulling out of the drive, pointing the car north, and leaving his home in his mirror.

Daniel had driven a good part of his journey before he pulled over to refuel and get a drink. He looked at the time and saw it was eleven. He wondered how the prom was going, wondered if Jamie was home early, wondered if he had found the letter on his bed. He checked his cell. There were no missed calls so he assumed Jamie wasn't home yet.

———

JAMIE LOOKED AT HIS WATCH. Eleven-thirty. The time had gone faster than he'd thought, and actually, the prom had been better than he thought it would be, so all in all a good night. He had danced with friends as much as his knee allowed. He'd shot the breeze with Tyler and April, had a few serious chats with friends, survived a confrontation with the whole senior football team, minus Greg, and stood at the back as Tyler and April were crowned prom king and queen, feeling proud of his friend, who was clearly besotted with his girl.

He had end-of-year chats with teachers and spent a long time talking to Mrs. Monroe, whom he thanked profusely for recommending him to the drama department at UCLA. She simply pulled him into a crushing hug, whispering in his ear how proud she was of him and how he would do well, simply because she said he would. It made him smile, and his heart filled with pride. It had been a good thing going to prom. He'd needed it. It ended things, and it allowed other things to start.

At just before midnight, he called a taxi, sharing it with Billy from the basketball team, who didn't quite know what to say to his ex-captain, despite being fairly inebriated from smuggled-in vodka. Billy was dropped off first, leaving Jamie to sit back in the cab, his eyes closed and excitement pulling at him. This was just the beginning of the rest of his life.

———

AT 12:19, Daniel finally reached the outskirts of Reno, the skyline of buildings dominating his vision, the anxiety in the pit of his stomach curling as he stopped at a Holiday Inn and booked himself in. He walked to the room, checking his cell for missed calls, then curled fully dressed on the bed, exhaustion claiming him almost immediately.

———

AT 12:25, Jamie arrived back home, and he smiled. He had

stuff to tell Dan, important life-changing decisions. The front door opened as he approached it, and his mom stood in the spilling light from the foyer. She smiled, but he started to feel apprehensive. Why wasn't Daniel at the door?

"Mom."

"Hello. Was it good?"

"Yeah, it was, better than I thought." He crossed the threshold, closing the door behind him, frowning. Still no Daniel.

"Is Dan in bed?" he asked

"Jamie darling, Daniel isn't here."

"Where is he?"

"He's gone to Nevada, to Reno, to his old home; he left a letter for you."

"He…" Jamie didn't know what to say. His heart pounded in his chest, and he felt sick. Had Daniel run, had he left? "He's gone… to…"

"To find his aunt, his mom's sister. He needed to go on his own, needed to get his head wrapped around the whole fostering business. He—"

"Did you know he was going?"

"We did; he took Mark's car."

"Mark knew he was going?" *I'm going to kill him.*

"Jamie, darling, go and read the letter. We'll be in the kitchen. When you're finished, come and talk."

Chapter Twenty-One

THE LETTER HAD BEEN LAID ON THE BED, SIMPLE IN A WHITE envelope, with *Jamie* written on the front in Daniel's sure strong script. It was odd to see the handwriting. He was so used to texting and emailing and instant messaging that seeing something handwritten was unique. He opened the envelope and pulled out a sheet of lined paper.

JAMIE, I know you are pissed with me at this moment, and I totally get why. I couldn't tell you I was going back because I know you would have wanted to come too, and I couldn't handle that. I can't have you here when I have so much to sort out.

I need to know why the rest of the family didn't want me and gave me up for fostering. I need to see where I came from, see if my cousins, you know, other stuff like that. Not that you aren't my real family, but then you know that.

That doesn't mean I don't want to hear from you though, so when you're done being pissed at me, can you phone me?

Please don't come out after me. I'll be back as soon as I have everything finished, okay?

Dan x

JAMIE RE-READ the letter five times, focusing on different things each time. Yes, he was pissed, more than pissed; he was furious. And, no, he couldn't see why Daniel had to do this alone.

Shit.

He was down the stairs in seconds, knee or no knee, sliding into the kitchen, bristling with righteous indignation.

"What the fuck, Mom?"

"Language, Jamie."

"He left us." *He left me.*

"He didn't leave us. He left to find his family."

"Well, they don't want him. Why would he do that? They could've come and gotten him at any time, and they didn't. He's happy here. I don't get it. Why—"

"Jamie, sit." This came from his dad, who could obviously see him winding up to a crescendo, anxiety and anger spinning out of control. Jamie didn't argue; he stopped talking and sat.

"Jamie darling, Daniel had his reasons. This thing you have between you—"

"Love, Mom," Jamie pointed out swiftly.

"Jamie, I'm not arguing with you. I'm not belittling you, or what you and Daniel have. Yes, it will be love to you, and yes, I realize how you feel, but whatever you have, Daniel still needed to do this Reno trip alone."

"He's too…" Jamie didn't know what to say. Jamie had always been there for Daniel, had been since his new brother had arrived. Daniel was vulnerable, shy, quiet, a geek; he wasn't confident. "He's too… he needs me to help him."

"No, Jamie, he doesn't, not this time. He's not the same. He changed when you were hurt. He's stronger, more determined, less needy."

"I'm really pissed at him," Jamie said stubbornly

"We know you are, and he wants us to get you to phone him. Will you phone him tonight?"

Jamie grimaced.

I'm not going to phone. I'm so cross, stupid freaking… No, I'm not going to phone him. He'll learn; he'll see why I'm so… "Yeah, I'll go do it now."

It was 1:15 by the time Jamie called. Daniel answered immediately.

"Jamie," he said breathlessly.

"Daniel, you are a complete fucking idiot." *There, that summed it up.*

"You read the letter," Daniel said hesitantly.

"I did, and I am so fucking angry with you, but shit, I suppose I understand. That doesn't make it any easier though and don't think I've forgiven you."

Daniel breathed a sigh of relief. "I am coming *home,* you know," he said softly, emphasizing the word home. "Reno will never be my home."

"I know you are, and if it isn't soon, I am driving out to get you."

"Want to maybe meet away from home when I have finished here? Maybe next weekend?"

"Away from here?"

"Yeah, away from family and home and people, just us."

"Whatdya have in mind?"

"Next Saturday evening. I've booked a room in this motel

in Shingletown, in my name. I'll text you the details. I'll be there at seven Saturday night. I promise."

"Shit, are we going to…" *Have sex? Make love? What?*

"Research, Jamie, do some research. I'm going to go. I'll talk to you tomorrow. I have my phone, and we can talk."

"I miss you already, you dumb fuck."

"Back at ya Jamie, back at ya."

PENGUINS. Cartoon penguins fucking… Jamie turned the laptop to one side. Okay that looked doable, but who would be the one…

Lube… Okay, lube was a good thing. It said so on every page he checked.

"Oh my God, I need bleach." Jamie was startled by his brother's voice, suddenly regretting that he hadn't locked his door.

"Ass," Jamie muttered succinctly.

"Jeez, bro, I come in to see my innocent little brother and this is what I see? Now I am scarred for life."

"Shouldn't be looking at my screen then."

"Is that a penguin?" Mark moved in closer and leaned over to look at the screen.

"Yeah."

"A male cartoon penguin doing the horizontal with another male cartoon penguin?"

"Yeah."

"Are there gay penguins?"

"Mark."

"Jesus, Jamie, that isn't going to help with the whole… thing. Here, give it to me."

Jamie tried to protest, but Mark was insistent, his tongue

poking out as he searched and clicked and searched some more, frowning as pop-ups littered the desktop, one thing Jamie was hoping to avoid.

"Mark, don't fuck with my—"

"Aha! All you need to know about the buttsex."

"Keep your voice down, dude."

"Here you go." Mark twisted the laptop back so Jamie could see. Jamie sighed as he closed down more pop-ups. "Graphics and words."

"Oh. My. God," Jamie swore and paled significantly.

"Lube… you'll need that, condoms, and ooooohh, the P-spot." Mark was really getting into this research.

"P-spot?" Jamie asked curiously. "What the hell is a P-spot?"

Mark pointed at the particular research he had pulled up, his eyebrows raising in interest. "Like the G-spot… Hmmm, never knew they had a name for it."

"Mark, no, please don't take notes."

"Dude," he said, affronted, "been there, done that."

"What?"

"I'm in college. Rachel and I have been together for like a year. You do the math."

"I can't think about that. I like Rachel, and my brain hurts."

Mark pulled the laptop back. "Here. Try this one, This is always a good one. See? There you go."

"Gay Sex Positions… For gay men… How to enjoy anal sex." This time Jamie really did pale.

"So, I'm getting a drink," Mark announced. "You want coffee?"

"Uh-huh," Jamie said, distracted. Pulling himself together, he took out his pad and pen so he could take notes and make a shopping list. Daniel would be proud. He took his time to make sure he had the correct page and then started the list.

Lube, check, condoms, check, but we're not going to need 'em 'cause we are taking this slow and… Jeez, is this picture even anatomically correct?

Jamie checked his cell again. He knew that today was the day Daniel was going to see his aunt to try to talk to her about everything, to try to get some idea of why he had been put into the foster system in the first place. Thank God he had been was all Jamie could think. Even though it was completely selfish. He knew the loss of his family had been an emotional burden Daniel still carried, but the thought of not having Daniel in his own life… impossible.

Still no message on the cell. Was that good news or bad news? He toyed with the idea of texting Daniel, but what if he was in the middle of… the middle of… whatever… with his aunt?

"Jamie." His mom was outside the door, and he scrambled to shut his laptop and tried to look innocent.

"Yes, Mom."

She opened the door and walked in. "Have you heard from Daniel?"

"Not since this morning."

"I hope he's okay," she said softly, nibbling at her lower lip and sitting down on the edge of the bed, sighing.

"Are you worried about him?"

"He'll be fine. He's grown up a lot in the last few days. Are you working on homework?"

"Yeah, er… history."

"Okay." She seemed distracted. "Let me know when you hear from him."

"Uh huh, I will, as soon as he calls."

"And Jamie?"

"Yeah."

"Don't go searching too deep. Porn will crash your computer."

THE PHARMACY RUN was like something out of Jamie's worst nightmare. He knew the girl behind the corner. She was in his AP math class. In fact, he was sure he had hit on her at some point.

Pulling his best I'm-heterosexual-really, horny teenage boy face, he found what he needed and sauntered up to the till.

"Jamie," the girl—Mitsy, Misty, Mindy—said wonderingly, taking the economy tube of slick and the condoms out of his hand and scanning them in.

"Hi." Hi was safe. He couldn't remember her name, and he didn't want to look stupid.

"Did you catch up to come back to AP math yet?"

"Yeah, Daniel has been getting me up to speed."

"Thirteen ninety-five."

He handed her the money, tension in his head getting worse. He could feel the blush starting from his neck and working its way up. *Come on, come on.* He watched as she placed it all in a bag and handed it over to him, not a trace of a smirk on her face. She gave no indication that the news Jamie was buying condoms and lube was going to make its way around the entire school by ten past nine on Monday.

"Thanks, bye."

"Bye, Jamie."

When he left the pharmacy, he ran. He ran all the way home, alternately embarrassed and excited. He really needed to get to his room; it was safe there.

Chapter Twenty-Two

DANIEL LOOKED DOWN AT THE ADDRESS IN HIS HAND, wondering if the information he had was even current. The house looked unassuming, matching many on the street. The gardens were tidy, children's toys littered the lawns, and it was a slice of perfect suburbia. Inside resided his aunt, his mom's sister, her husband of twenty years, Ian, and her three children, Louise, his age, Anthony, who was eleven, and Helena, only four. His cousins. His only family, for all he knew, his research not showing much more. He remembered his Aunt Julia vaguely. He knew she and his mom weren't close, knew there had been some sort of falling out, but he didn't know the details.

He had been sitting in the Toyota for half an hour, just watching, and knew he had to move soon or be labeled as a stalker. He had deliberately arranged this visit during a school day. He had only his aunt to face. He wasn't sure he could handle cousins as yet.

Courage, he needed courage. He needed to text Jamie, despite the fact he knew he would be in school prepping for finals next week. He pulled out his cell.

. . .

DANIEL: Outside house, not sure what I'm going to say.

JAMIE: SAY, "I'M DANIEL" :-)

DANIEL: Useful, J. thanks for that ((

JAMIE: In history, sheet of stuff for finals. Can't text. Evans is a dick.

DANIEL: Wish me luck?

JAMIE: Good luck, text me x

DANIEL PUT his cell back in his pocket and breathed deeply. Time to do this. He climbed out of the car, scanning the area, and purposefully walked up the path to the door. He knocked, hearing music inside and the sounds of the television, and he focused on the noises, trying to calm himself down. It startled him when the door was thrown open; his breath hitched in his throat. A woman stood in the open doorway, dressed in flowing colors and jeans. She looked so much like his mom it made him take a step back. Julia.

She smiled briefly, looking behind him, her head to one side. He didn't know what to say, and then she looked directly at him.

"Oh my God," she whispered, her hand going to her mouth. "Daniel?"

"Aunt Julia?"

Suddenly remembering her manners, she stood to one side, gesturing him inside. "Come in, come in, Daniel. Oh God, it's been…"

"Eight years since the funeral," Daniel stated simply.

"Eight years… eight years." She led him through to the kitchen, indicating he should sit at the table as she busied herself with mugs. "Have you been to see the graves? Do you know where they are? We take the children and go every birthday and at Christmas, make sure they are being looked after. I never see flowers from you, but I imagine we go on the nearest weekend so maybe not on the actual day. I can give you directions… How long are you in Reno? Is this a long stay? Your cousins will be pleased to meet you. Louise is eighteen next month, but then that means you were eighteen in March…"

Daniel watched as she made coffee and talked a mile a minute, about everything and nothing, so different from his mom. There had been twelve years between the two sisters. He remembered Christmas gatherings… two such different families, Louise a typical tomboy, forever covered in mud and muck, always earning a disapproving glare from Daniel's mom. Daniel's mom so very proud of her perfect, talented, and perpetually clean son. He'd hated those gatherings. If anything, they'd made him retreat more into his music, which was fine, as his mom did like to make him perform on a regular basis.

Julia had stopped talking and was looking at him with concern, an air of apprehension about her.

"Daniel?" she asked softly… why are you here… what do you want?

Daniel wanted to wait to ask. He wanted to meet his family before he destroyed any possible relationship with them by asking awkward questions, wanted one last time to feel a connection that was his by blood.

I'm going to wait. I'm not just going to spring it on her. I can't. It will ruin everything. I'm going to have to…

"Why didn't you keep me?"

Well, shit.

Julia swallowed, her face pale, and sat at the table opposite him.

"I don't know what to say. I had post-partum depression with Anthony. I wasn't brave enough. I didn't think I could cope with your special needs."

"Special needs."

"You were special, Daniel, gifted, talented, and I was a coward. My head was so full of myself, and then later when I was better, you were happy, Daniel. You were happy with your new family."

"How did you know?"

"We had reports, no, not reports, letters, lovely letters from your foster mom, Mrs. Walker, every year, letting us know. Always saying you needed your real family to know you, but I never even wrote back. I couldn't. I had so much to say sorry for, and I didn't know where to start."

"I was happy. I *am* happy, but…"

"But?"

"Do you know… Can you even begin to see… to understand…"

"No, I can't. I can't understand. I had lost a sister, lost a sister to suicide. She didn't talk to me; she didn't tell me… I didn't see. But you lost your dad and then your mom… so close… and I should have been there for you."

There was a long pause with Julia waiting for Daniel to

comment, to agree, to disagree, anything. "You should have been there, if only just so I knew you were there, that I hadn't done some awful thing that made you hate me."

Julia looked stricken. "Is that what you thought? Daniel, is that what you thought?"

Daniel just nodded. He could feel a choking emotion rising in him, and he didn't want to have a panic attack now, here, in his aunt's kitchen.

"Daniel, you did nothing wrong. How could you ever think that?"

"Julia… Aunt Julia… my dad died, my mom left me by killing herself. I wasn't worth her holding onto life for, and then you, when everything was finished, when I left that cemetery, you couldn't even look at me. You didn't want me." Daniel could feel the panic rising. He really needed to leave; he stood.

"Daniel, please don't go. I want to explain, to say sorry, to get to know you again?" She was pleading, but the air was tight in his lungs.

"I need to… air," he said, his fingers pushing desperately against his breast bone, his eyes wide as he stumbled to the front door, feeling Julia trying to pull him back, pulling him. Pushing out of the door, he gulped in fresh air.

"Daniel."

"Mom?"

"Louise, get some water."

"Mom, what the—"

"Water. Daniel? Daniel?"

"Daniel?"

"I'M FINE, HONESTLY."

Louise sat down next to him, touching his arm and pressing lightly. "I know you are. It's just the shock and stuff," she said helpfully. Daniel looked into gray eyes. His smile rueful, he held out his hand.

"Daniel," he said, introducing himself softly. She looked down at his hand then pulled him in for a hug instead, chuckling into his ear.

"I know your name, doofus. How about we go back indoors, eh?"

It was all Daniel could do to nod, a smile pushing its way through the tears that were threatening to force their way out.

JAMIE_SOLO: hey, you there?

810Daniel: only just

Jamie_Solo: and?

810Daniel: not bad, met cousin and mum's sister, Julia

Jamie_Solo: and?

810Daniel: hard, really hard, they had their reasons tho :-(

Jamie_Solo: wanna talk?

810Daniel: nah, not so much

Jamie_Solo: we still meeting?

810Daniel: don't you wanna?

Jamie_Solo: god yeah, I got something today

810Daniel: what

Jamie_Solo: just stuff

810Daniel: stuff

Jamie_Solo: stuff we need

810Daniel: stuff

Jamie_Solo: hahaha

810Daniel: is your cell charged

Jamie_Solo: yeah

810Daniel: wanna have phone sex?

Jamie_Solo: Signing off :-)

JAMIE CALLED DANIEL. It was wonderful to hear his boyfriend's voice.

"I don't get it though," Jamie offered gently, his voice soft and insistent across the miles. He had told his mom that Daniel was okay and then locked himself in his room, leaning back on his bed, listening as Daniel explained his day

"What?" Daniel asked. "What don't you get?"

"Mom writing letters to Julia all this time."

"That's Mom, Jamie. She always tries to do the right thing."

"Yeah, suppose so."

"What you wearing?" Daniel said to change the subject.

"You are joking with me." Jamie suddenly felt nervous.

"What are you wearing?" Damn, Daniel was insistent.

"Daannnn," Jamie whined

"Jamie."

"Jeez, sweats." Nothing remotely sexy or hot.

"And?" Jamie could hear the leering quality in Daniel's voice across the miles.

"And nothing. Nothing else, m'ready for bed."

"Is it Saturday yet?" Daniel finally laughed.

"Not long, Dan, not long."

Chapter Twenty-Three

DANIEL WAS BACK IN THE CAR BY ELEVEN SATURDAY morning, feeling warm and positive from his good-byes with his Nevada family. His ears rang with promises of meeting up in the summer, emails, and phone calls. They exchanged all forms of communication information.

He hadn't fully come to terms with everything yet though. He needed to do some more talking, some more thinking, learn more about his extended family, and come to understand Julia's reasoning. But he felt that, at least, he was making some progress and looking forward to the future.

Not least of which was meeting Jamie at the motel. Jamie was already on his way. He had texted that he had left home.

The next text summarized Jamie's crappy bus journey:

Dude you are so lucky with the Toyota.

The next one came in several minutes later.

Room is in the name of Keyes, right? Not Walker?

And the one after that:

Shit, this room is pink, pink!

The last one:

Showered and naked, where are you?

Daniel knew the room, knew Jamie would have the key, so he went straight there. It was six fifty-five exactly, and he was tired from the journey but energized as soon as the garish pink outside hit his eyes.

He knocked, and seconds later, the door opened, a grinning, but dressed, Jamie pulling him into the room and into such a normal Jamie-hug Daniel barely able to breathe. His boyfriend attempted to steal a kiss, but Daniel pushed him away laughing.

"Shower, I need a shower and to brush my teeth. Give me five, yeah?" Daniel said with a smile. Jamie grimaced, and Daniel smirked, backing away from Jamie and crossing to the bathroom.

"I thought you were going to be naked," Daniel called over his shoulder and shut the bathroom door. He stripped quickly, turning the tap and adjusting the water. He liked the temperature way hotter than Jamie, often a bone of contention if he grabbed a shower first. Mostly it caused much bickering followed by much swearing from the shared bathroom.

He wasn't even in the shower yet when the bathroom door opened and a totally naked Jamie stood inside the door. Daniel swallowed, willing himself to wait until after the shower, eyes fixed on Jamie's as he climbed into the shower and started to soak his body. Daniel knew what his own body looked like. He had the softer curves of a bookworm, a studier who hated most sports. Jamie used to have the slim, toned physique of a player, but since the attack, he had softened a little. It added a healthy roundness to his face and made his dimples deeper.

"Tiny steps," Jamie said more to himself than to Daniel and leaned back against the doorframe. Half of Daniel wanted Jamie to jump in the shower with him. The other half admitted he wouldn't know what to do when Jamie got there.

"I'll be out in a minute," Daniel shouted over the noise of the shower.

"Hurry up." Jamie said firmly. Jamie was evidently totally at ease naked in front of Daniel, but Daniel really wasn't there just yet. He climbed out of the shower and pulled a towel to dry his hair so it stood up in soft spikes. Then he methodically brushed his teeth, rinsing and repeating until he felt fresh. "Finished," he said smiling. Finally, he held out his hand. Jamie grasped it and pulled him back into the bedroom.

This is not weird. This is not weird. This is not weird. The words were on repeat in Daniel's head.

"Daniel, can we talk before we do anything?"

"Uh-huh," Daniel agreed, pushing Jamie back onto the bed and climbing over him to draw him into a sloppy open-mouthed kiss.

"I've been…" *kiss* "… looking at some…" *kiss* "… websites and I'm…" *kiss* "… not keen on the…" *kiss* "… whole anal…" *kiss* "… thing."

"Uh-huh." Daniel was still kissing and holding and stroking Jamie's face. His left elbow supported his weight, his right hand stroking from throat to temple, tracing a pattern over Jamie's heated skin.

"I don't think I'm ready for any of that," Daniel said softly. "I just want to learn stuff slowly. So can I touch you?" Daniel's hand moved lower to trace around Jamie's hard nipple, pulling on the nub, twisting gently.

Lightning traveled straight to his dick, and he stopped moving. Caressing Jamie was enough to near bring himself off. Just being able to touch and to feel was more than enough in his head to push him close to coming embarrassingly fast. He realized Jamie's hands weren't moving. He was gripping the bedclothes.

"Are you okay?" Daniel asked gently. He wasn't going to do anything Jamie didn't want.

"I think the whole research thing freaked me out. Can we just…" He groaned into Daniel's mouth.

"Anything," Daniel breathed. He moved his hand lower, twisting into the curls at the base of Jamie's dick. God, how he wanted to touch Jamie there, drag his hands to the tip of him then swallow him down. "We can go slow." His hormones were making a liar of him. But if Jamie wanted to stop, then Daniel would in a heartbeat.

"I want you to… Daniel."

Daniel wasn't sure what Jamie wanted as his boyfriend never finished the sentence.

"Your hands on me. Please, Jamie," Daniel begged. His breath was short and harsh into an almost endless kiss. Daniel was giving Jamie the choice to take this as far as he wanted.

The plea galvanized Jamie into action, and he twisted and pulled Daniel to lie flat on him. Daniel's hand was trapped between them, and Jamie's dick was rubbing at Daniel's hip bone, thrusting hard against him.

"Jamie… I'm so close." Daniel couldn't pull together any more words that made any sense in his head. Jamie was laughing; slow and low, it was a chuckle of near glee, then Jamie's hand was pulling, twisting, and searching. It was the most erotic thing Daniel had ever felt. With Jamie naked under and against him, he felt his orgasm building in the base of his spine, flooding his heated blood with need. Jeez, he was going to shoot. They needed to… slow… down.

"I'm going to… we've gotta." Jamie seemed as close as he was if his strangled words were any indication, and suddenly, Daniel knew what he needed.

"Jamie, let it happen."

Jamie lost it, and white heat spread from Daniel's head to

his toes. Jamie was arched up against Daniel, and Daniel was hearing and feeling the release—a gasp, a groan and a sigh. One word. Daniel. It was too much, and Daniel was coming so hard he forgot to breathe. When he remembered, his first inhalation was accompanied by a torrent of mixed feelings that washed over him from his very core. He was so happy to be here with Jamie on day one of the rest of their lives, but this last week had been so hard.

"I've missed you so much, Jamie," he said brokenly. "I've missed you so much. This week, fuck, I can't stop." Trying to stop the choked emotion in his throat, he focused hard on the scar on Jamie's chest, the raised pink skin a reminder of his boyfriend's pain.

"Daniel? You can't stop what?"

"I can't stop feeling like this is all going to be taken away from me," he admitted finally. Tears stuck heavy and sticky in his voice.

Jamie pulled him close, wrapping his arms around him. Oblivious to the mess between them, Daniel clung to Jamie and took every ounce of strength he could from him.

This had been one hell of a week.

One hell of a life.

JAMIE FINALLY ENCOURAGED them to separate when the cold and damp pushed its way through the neediness of contact and made them roll off the bed. Jamie led Daniel by the hand to the bathroom, turning back briefly just to check that he was okay. Daniel looked a long way past tired, his eyes red rimmed from the crying. He also looked somehow relaxed and loose, and he seemed more than happy to let Jamie pull him about. One-handed, Jamie started running the water and encouraging Daniel into the shower, propping him up against the tile and lathering up his hands. He soaped Daniel across the chest, over the shoulders, around his neck, massaging his flat stomach with soothing gentling strokes. He locked his hands around Daniel's back, pulling him tight then using his height advantage to tilt back Daniel's head and push in for a heated open-mouthed kiss.

"I love you, Daniel," Jamie said fiercely. "I love you."

Daniel smiled and arched his neck as Jamie continued a path of small bites and licks and sucks up his neck, pulling him in for a quick kiss. "I love you too," he said simply.

Epilogue

THE MORNING OF GRADUATION WAS CALM AND PEACEFUL. Even with the school time Jamie had missed he had more than enough credits to graduate. He and Jamie both stood at the front door, allowing the photos and the fussing from a moist-eyed Mom and a gruff-sounding Dad.

Mark smirked… a lot.

Megan was twirling in front of them in her prettiest dress, visibly shivering with excitement, her long chestnut hair loose down her back. Her brothers were having a special day, and she was part of them. It was the most exciting day of her life so far.

Jamie was hopping—there was no other word for it—from foot to foot under his robe, but it was only Daniel who could feel the movement, and he simply reached a hand across and held Jamie's tightly, an action not missed by Mark, who stopped smirking and started to look concerned.

"Are you going to be doing that today?" He waved vaguely at the boys' joined hands.

Daniel shook his head. "I'm not ready for that," he said softly, his eyes on Jamie, who seemed to slump in relief.

"Me neither," he said simply, squeezing Daniel's hand tightly.

"S'just if you are, I wanna know, so I can be there if the shit hits the fan," Mark pointed out.

"You're not going to be there forever," Jamie said. "One day people will know, but we'll deal with it."

"Well, given we are on the same campus, I'm not going to be far," Mark insisted. Jamie smiled gratefully, knowing that, yes, Mark was okay with all this and he would do the big brother thing if he needed.

"You ready, boys?" Dad asked, lifting the car keys and opening the front door.

One last squeeze of the hand.

"As we'll ever be." Jamie laughed and walked down the three small steps outside the front door, looking back from the bottom and throwing a smile of pure Jamie. It went straight to Daniel's heart.

It wouldn't be the graduation he remembered when he looked back years from now.

It would be this single moment of innocent perfection as Jamie grinned up at him, the boy he was unashamedly happy and in love with, shadows of the man he would become around him.

It would be enough of a memory to last a lifetime.

Daniel knew that.

———

AT GRADUATION, it finally hit Jamie what was happening next.

College.

They had a shared room in the dorms with all the associated promise that gave. The promise of being together.

Alone. It alternately worried and pleased Jamie to think about what it would bring.

Every time he worried, he realized he unconsciously traced the raised scar on his chest, and every single time Daniel noticed him do this, a shadow would pass across his face, his gray eyes clouding and concern twisting his mouth. Jamie would snap out of his worries. What if they ended up getting on each other's nerves and ended up hating each other? What if people hated what they were? There were going to be a lot of boys at college. What if one of them stole Daniel away? What if Daniel didn't love him but wanted someone else?

"Stop it, Jamie," Daniel said one sunny Saturday morning. Both boys lay sprawled under the hoop. For the first time since the injuries, Jamie had beaten Daniel. Finally he was getting some strength back in his knee. It had been a close game, and Daniel had played to win. Every time they had gone one-on-one since Jamie had been given the all clear to play limited sports, Daniel had played to win. This made Jamie's five-four victory meaningful and much needed.

"Stop what?" Jamie finally answered.

"Stop worrying. There is nothing we can do to change how college will be for us. We just have to be us. Jamie and Daniel, Daniel and Jamie."

"Yeah, I know."

"It will be fine. We'll deal with things together."

"I just… sometimes I get… I dunno…"

"Scared?"

"Yeah, I 'spose. Scared kind of sums it up."

"About us?"

"Shit no," Jamie lied. He didn't want to talk about his fears that Daniel would leave him. "About people," he continued, "and what they think."

"Really. I don't give a shit what people think," Daniel said forcefully.

"See, I get scared we will come up against people like Lucy and Greg, and they will want to hurt us…" Again his hand went to his scar. Daniel leaned over and traced the scar through the sweat-soaked T-shirt and winced.

"There will always be Gregs and Lucys, Jamie. We just have to make sure we stay strong and stay careful. I mean we could always—"

"No."

"You didn't know what I was going to say."

"I did. You were going to say we could always stay apart, not do this thing. Or something equally stupid."

Daniel looked affronted, but Jamie knew that was exactly what Daniel had been going to say.

"I wasn't—"

"Bullshit. I know you."

"Okay, okay, but jeez, things would be easier, and you wouldn't get hurt."

"Let's make a deal. We'll push our worrying to one side. There is no way I would ever let go of what we have here because something might happen."

Mark's voice broke through their discussion. "Girls," he said smirking, forever with the big-brother smirking. He slumped down on the grass next to them. "I'm leaving tonight, so wanted to say I'll see ya' in the dorm." He didn't move to leave though, instead lying back on the grass and looking up at the cloudless California sky.

Daniel and Jamie copied him until they were all lying back, reliving memories of other summers and other days where they'd stared at the sky as boys, the endless blue promising so much.

"Saw you out here, bro," Mark started simply. "You beat Shorty."

Jamie heard an element of pride in his voice. "Easy," Jamie responded. He winced as he moved his knee. Maybe not as easy as it used to be, but hey, he'd finally beat Daniel.

"Yeah, right," Daniel snorted. "Easy, my ass."

"Please don't start conversations that feature your ass," Mark said. He punched Daniel's arm, but Daniel just grinned.

"So college then," Jamie started. "Tell us more."

"Well, shit, dude." Mark laughed. "The girls. It's all about the girls."

Daniel looked at him and then Jamie. Jamie could tell what he was thinking, and he was so up on that plan. They both moved at the same time, their combined weight landing on Mark in one go.

Mark was so going to pay for that comment.

THE END

Also by RJ Scott

Single Dads

Single | Today | Promise | Always (Apr 2020) | Listen (July 2020)

Lancaster Falls

What Lies Beneath | Without a Trace (Jan 2020) | All that Remains (Mar 2020)

Texas

The Heart of Texas | Texas Winter | Texas Heat | Texas Family | Texas Christmas | Texas Fall | Texas Wedding | Texas Gift | Home For Christmas

Legacy (spin-off from Texas series)

Kyle | Gabriel | Daniel

Montana

Crooked Tree Ranch | The Rancher's Son | A Cowboy's Home | Snow In Montana | Second Chance Ranch | Montana Sky

Wyoming

Winter Cowboy | Summer Drifter

Action Adventure Romance

Heroes, Bodyguards, First Responders, SEALs, Marines, Cops

Sanctuary

Guarding Morgan | The Only Easy Day | Face Value | Still Waters |
Full Circle | The Journal of Sanctuary 1 | World's Collide |
Accidental Hero | Ghost | By The Numbers

A Reason To Stay | Last Marine Standing | Deacon's Law

Bodyguards Inc

Bodyguard to a Sex God | The Ex-Factor | Max and the Prince |
Undercover Lovers | Love's Design | Kissing Alex

Standalone

Alpha Delta | Seth & Casey

All The King's Men | Retrograde | Force of Nature

Hockey Romance

Standalone Titles

Secrets | Dallas Christmas | Last Chance

Hockey Romance written with V.L. Locey

Harrisburg Railers

Changing Lines | First Season | Deep Edge | Poke Check| Last Defense | Goal Line | Neutral Zone | Hat Trick | Save the Date

Owatonna U

Ryker | Scott | Benoit

Arizona Raptors

Coast To Coast

Small Town / First Responders Romance

Ellery Mountain

The Fireman and the Cop | The Teacher and the Soldier | The Carpenter and the Actor | The Doctor and the Bad Boy | The Paramedic and the Writer | The Barman and the SEAL | The Agent and the Model | The Sinner and the Saint

---

Christmas Romance

The Christmas Throwaway | Love Happens Anyway | New York Christmas | The Christmas Collection | Jesse's Christmas | The Road to Frosty Hollow | Christmas Prince | Dallas Christmas | Angel in a Book Shop | Mr Sparkles

Paranormal Romance

Standalone Stories

The Gallows Tree | The New Wolf | The Soldier's Tale | Ghost In The Stone (Coming Halloween 2019)

In the Shadow of the Wolf

With Diane Adams

Shattered Secrets | Broken Memories | Splintered Lies

Oracle

Oracle | Book of Secrets | The Oracle Collection

End Street Detective Agency

With Amber Kell

End Street Volume 1 (Cupid Curse / Wicked Wolf) | End Street Volume 2 (Dragon's Dilemma / Sinful Santa) | End Street Volume 3 (Purple Pearl / Guilty Ghost)

Kingdom

Kingdom Volume 1 (Vampire Contract, Guilty Werewolf, Warlock's Secret) | Kingdom Volume 2 (Demon's Blood, Incubus Agenda, Third Kingdom)

Fire

Meet RJ Scott

RJ is the author of the over one hundred published novels and discovered romance in books at a very young age. She realized that if there wasn't romance on the page, she could create it in her head, and is a lifelong writer. She lives and works out of her home in the beautiful English countryside, spends her spare time reading, watching films, and enjoying time with her family. The last time she had a week's break from writing she didn't like it one little bit and has yet to meet a bottle of wine she couldn't defeat.

www.rjscott.co.uk | rj@rjscott.co.uk

I'm an APP!
Go to app.rjscott.co.uk on your phone
and never miss another release!

facebook.com/author.rjscott

twitter.com/Rjscott_author

instagram.com/rjscott_author

bookbub.com/authors/rj-scott

pinterest.com/rjscottauthor